I0561032

George Franklin Hall

A Study in Bloomers, or, The Model New Woman

A novel

George Franklin Hall

A Study in Bloomers, or, The Model New Woman
A novel

ISBN/EAN: 9783337000233

Printed in Europe, USA, Canada, Australia, Japan

Cover: Foto ©Andreas Hilbeck / pixelio.de

More available books at **www.hansebooks.com**

THE NEW WOMAN IN HUNTING COSTUME.

A STUDY

IN

BLOOMERS

OR

THE MODEL NEW WOMAN.

A NOVEL BY

GEORGE F. HALL.

AUTHOR OF "PLAIN POINTS."

"GRACE WAS IN ALL HER STEPS, HEAVEN IN HER EYE,
IN EVERY GESTURE DIGNITY AND LOVE."--MILTON.

AMERICAN BIBLE HOUSE:
CHICAGO, PHILADELPHIA, STOCKTON.
1895.

Copyrighted 1895

BY

LINCOLN W. WALTER.

———————

All Rights Reserved,

CONTENTS.

LIST OF ILLUSTRATIONS.

LIST OF ILLUSTRATIONS.

HERE ARE GIRLS WHO CAN PADDLE THEIR OWN
CANOE.

SUBJECTS DISCUSSED.

DRESS REFORM.   RELIGION.   MARRIAGE.

DIETETICS.   CO-EDUCATION.   SOCIETY.

EQUAL SUFFRAGE.   RACE QUESTION.   DIVORCE.

PROHIBITION.   ATHLETICS.   BIMETALISM.

TOBACCO-SMOKING.   MODERATE DRINKING.

REFERENCES.

BURROWS.	INGALLS.	ROSSETTI.
BROOKS.	JOB.	RUSKIN.
BURKE.	JONSON.	ROGERS.
BEETHOVEN.	KELLOGG.	SHAKESPEARE
COWPERTHWAIT.	KITCHEN.	SIGOURNEY.
CAESAR.	LISTZ.	ST. JOHN.
CINDERELLA.	LONGFELLOW.	STANDARD.
DEPEW.	LEWIS.	SEWARD.
DORR.	LEOPOLD.	SHELLEY.
DIX.	LIVESEY.	SUMNER.
DAVID.	LINCOLN.	STOWE.
ECOB.	LOWBER.	SIDNEY.
ELLIS.	LOWELL.	SOLOMON.
GOETHE.	MACAULAY.	SWIFT.
GARFIELD.	MILLER.	THOMSON.
GREELEY.	MULOCK.	TENNYSON.
GOLDSMITH.	MADAME DE STAEL.	TAYLOR.
GLADSTONE	NAPOLEON.	WHITTIER.
HOLLAND.	OUSELEY.	WILLARD.
HAYES.	PAUL.	WEBSTER.
HOOD.	PHILLIPS.	WASHINGTON.
HAVERGAL.	PAYNE.	ZOLA.

A STUDY IN BLOOMERS.

A STUDY IN BLOOMERS.

CHAPTER I.

MY OUTING AT SPRING ROCK VILLA.

"I know a spot where the wild vines creep,
   And the coral moss-cups grow,
And where at the foot of the rocky steep,
   The sweet blue violets grow."
         —JULIA C. R. DORR.

It was the fifth day of August, 1895. The summer weeks had been excessively hot, and I was beginning to feel worn and languid. Although but twenty-five and unmarried, I looked like an over-worked professional man of middle age, who had long had the cares of a large family and the drawbacks of a small salary on his mind. And yet I was perfectly free from wedlock, with no prospects, and my salary was four thousand a year—very good for a young man only three years out of college. I was pastor of a large and influential Chicago church, and, although very pleasant, my work was very exacting. Hence I always looked forward anxiously to a six weeks' vacation each year, which my people were good enough to allow.

"And where are you going this year, Doctor?" had been asked me so many times the past fortnight that the clouds, and trees, and express wagons seemed to be echoing and re-echoing the query. As usual, it had been a difficult matter to decide, for there are so many nice resorts in this grand country of ours. But I had finally concluded to spend the weeks quietly at Spring Rock Villa, a beautiful country seat in Northern Wisconsin, owned by one of my parishoners, a wealthy banker. The family had very kindly invited me to be their guest for the summer, and I am a thousand times glad I accepted the invitation, for it was there that I first saw the sweet girl in bloomers who has transformed my life in more ways than one.

After a somewhat tedious ride, I found myself at my journey's end. It was evening, and, after a hearty meal and luxurious bath, I retired. A good night's rest, and I was ready to relish the bewildering beauty of nature that everywhere presented itself. Spring Rock Villa embraced several hundred acres, including a well-stocked farm. The buildings were all modern, but unique in their architecture. The grounds were exquisitely laid out, and cared for by an experienced gardener from the old country. Just back of the villa were the hills, in which abounded game of

all kinds, and from which flowed a laughing stream.
A lake hard by, covering a thousand acres, with
sandy, pebbly shores and water clear as crystal, com-
pleted the picture. Smithville, a town of 3,000 people, with excellent railroad connections and all modern improvements, was only five miles away. Hence
from every standpoint of consideration, Spring Rock
Villa seemed to me an ideal place in which to take
one's outing.

I don't like watering places for vacation purposes.
There is too much buzz, and flurry, and sham. Give
me some quiet spot where nature has done her best
to provide every means of enjoyment, and where society has not yet secured a monopoly.

"Well, Doctor, we want you to make yourself at
home while here," said genial Banker Brown after
breakfast. "There are some good saddle horses in
the stable if you wish to ride. Or, you can take a
round on the lake in the electric boat if you prefer.
Do you ride a wheel?"

"No, I do not. That's one fad I've never adopted,
Mr. Brown," said I. "There's an old saying that it's
better to be out of the world than out of fashion; but
I've gotten along very well thus far without a bicycle, and I think I shall try and complete my course
wheelless."

"But have you gotten along so well, Doctor?" said
Mrs. Brown. "It seems to me that you are looking
quite thin. Perhaps if you had spent two or three

hours daily on a bicycle during the season you would be stronger to-day."

"Really, Mrs. Brown, do you think bicycle riding beneficial to the health?"

"I cannot speak from experience," said the amiable lady, "but the testimony of many of my friends who are devoted to their wheels is all on one side of the question. Now there is Grace Thorne, for instance. Mr. Brown remembers that when she first came to Smithville, four summers ago, she was pale and weak; but now she is one of the handsomest creatures I ever saw, and as strong as an ox, apparently. You should see her spinning along the lane in her bloomers, Doctor. She is a perfect picture of health and female loveliness if I ever saw one."

"Bloomers?" I gasped. "Mrs. Brown!"

The banker and his wife laughed heartily at my expense. And then we calmly discussed the bloomer question. To my amazement Mrs. Brown, whom I had always considered one of the most exemplary ladies of my parish, was an all-round enthusiast on the new woman hobby. But Mr. Brown shared my conservatism. We seriously questioned the womanliness of bicycle riding at all on the part of the gentler sex, much less the wearing of bloomers.

"I am certainly surprised," said my hostess, "that you should be opposed to progress, Doctor. Why, the bicycle is one of the greatest hygienic inventions of this century. It has already accomplished won-

AN IDEAL PLACE IN WHICH TO TAKE ONE'S OUTING.
—Page 21.

ders for both sexes, and I feel confident that its day of usefulness has only dawned. It stands for broader shoulders, firmer muscles and more powerful chests. To me a shining wheel suggests a glow of health. Were I not so old I should have a bicycle before Saturday night."

"Your enthusiasm is invigorating, Mrs. Brown," said I. "But do not learned physicians condemn the wheel, especially for women?"

"Oh, yes. Learned physicians condemn everything, some of them. But there are physicians and physicians. I do not think it can be proven that the highest medical authorities are against bicycling for women. How dare they in the face of facts? You know that Gil Blas says 'Facts are stubborn things,' and the facts are that the wheel is proving an inestimable boon to woman. But come, Doctor, we can argue at some other time. You are doubtless anxious to take a stroll through the hills, so we will not detain you longer. We lunch at one; or, if you prefer to carry a little lunch with you, and not return till later in the day, I will instruct the butler to prepare a basket for you."

"Thank you, Mrs. Brown. I believe I'll take a lunch and spend the day in the hills."

And so, basket in hand, and a gun on my shoulder, I started for the wilds of nature. I was not much of a hunter, but nevertheless liked the sport of an occasional shot. During the day I bagged a few squirrels and quails. At noon I found a pleasant nook far up among the hills, and deep in the recesses of rocks and trees. There by a cool, sparkling spring I sat down and enjoyed my lunch. With only a bird dog for a companion, I thus spent many a pleasant day, till I had grown quite strong. My skin was as brown as a berry, and my appetite as vigorous as a harvester's. Freed from the busy cares of life, my jaded energies were speedily rejuvenated, and being became a pleasure rather than a task. An annual vacation is a religious duty.

Three weeks had flown by, and, although we had had numerous discussions, Mrs. Brown had not yet convinced me as to the utility of bicycles, nor the beauty of bloomers.

"Just wait till you see Grace Thorne," she had said several times, "and you will undergo a change of heart."

Miss Thorne was the daughter of a well-to-do tradesman in Smithville, where she was the idol of the town, because of her many excellent qualities and deeds of mercy. At least Mrs. Brown said so. But I feared she might be mistaken in this, as in the question of wheels and bloomers. Miss Thorne, although but twenty-four, was a leader among her sex in Smithville, and had been sent to Boston as a delegate to some sort of a reform convention just a day before my arrival at the villa. She had tarried a few days in Ohio to visit relatives on her return home-

AND SO, BASKET IN HAND, AND A GUN ON MY
SHOULDED, I STARTED FOR THE WILDS OF NA-
TURE.—Page 25.

ward, and hence the delay. Mrs. Brown was her intimate friend, and it was with no little interest that
I finally began to look for her advent. As to match-
making, I well knew that my kind hostess had no de-
signs, for she was above such contemptuous foolish-
ness. It would have done little good anyhow, for I
felt myself to be woman-proof. I had had several
little love experiences in college, and had become
hardened. I was sure that I was wedded to my profession, and did not care for any other bride.

It was Tuesday evening. I was just returning
from a day on the lake. With fishing tackle, and a
nice mess of bass, I was plodding carelessly down the
lane, when what should I see but a bicyclist ap-
proaching from the direction of Smithville. And she
was dressed in bloomers! Often on the boulevards
in Chicago I had observed similar sights, but always
with a feeling that my good sense of the delicate had
been outraged. But not so this time. The lady ap-
proaching was soon beside me, and in a moment had
passed on, her bright wheel spinning her along at the
rate of ten miles or so an hour. Above the average in
height, well rounded in form, with snowy neck and
rosy cheeks, whoever it was, she presented a vision of
loveliness, thought I. And I was not long in concluding that if that were Miss Thorne, I should like
to make her acquaintance right soon, bloomers or no
bloomers.

I quickened my pace and was soon at the villa.

Depositing my game with the butler, I repaired to my room, attired myself for dinner, and innocently made my way to the parlor.

"Ah, Doctor, I did not know that you had arrived," said Mrs. Brown. "Allow me to present you to my friend, Miss Thorne, Rev. Dr. Charlton."

To my utter bewilderment, the fair young lady was still attired in her bloomers. I do not know just how I had expected her to make a change, for certainly our hostess, being a very stout old lady, could not have supplied her with a suitable gown; and yet I expected to see her in a different garb from the one worn on the wheel. But, no; there she sat in bloomers of the regulation pattern. The offensive costume was made of rich, dark velvet, cut quite full, and gathered neatly just below the knee, thus leaving exposed a plump calf and delicately moulded ankle, for the boots were low-cut, and there were no leggings. The waist was made of changeable silk, with the usual large sleeves. Save a little diamond which scintillated at her pretty neck, and a single ring on her left third finger, she wore no ornaments. A heavy fold of dark brown hair was coyously draped over each little pink ear, while from beneath long lashes a pair of deep blue eyes shot glances of penetrating intelligence. Verily here was a typical woman of the new school, and before we had conversed long I found myself absorbingly interested. I forgot all about her bloomers, until we arose to go out to dinner. With

THE OFFENSIVE COSTUME WAS MADE OF RICH,
DARK VELVET, CUT QUITE FULL AND GATHERED
NEATLY AT THE KNEE.--Page 30.

sensations better imagined than described, I stilled my prejudice and offered my arm. So accustomed all my life to heavy skirts and long trails, I felt almost like apologizing for being in the presence of a woman who seemed only half dressed. And yet there was something that said to my inner consciousness, This is all very sensible and very nice. Five feet eight if an inch, one hundred and fifty pounds if an ounce, perfectly proportioned, and as light on her feet as a feather—to walk beside her gave me a peculiar sense of exalted manhood. Instinctively I reasoned to myself, why cannot all women be so? It seems so much better than to be little, and pale, and doll-like. I had always imagined that the new woman must be indelicate; but here was a woman as delicate as anybody's sister dare be, and yet apparently strong enough to wrestle with a giant.

As the meal progressed the conversation turned from fishing tackle, guns, and dogs, to bicycling and dress reform. It was a hobby with Mrs. Brown, and as her fair guest had just returned from a great new-woman convention, it was very natural that we should all discuss the subject.

"And you are still as much in love with your bicycle as ever, Miss Thorne?" inquired Mr. Brown, with a side glance full of merriment.

"Oh, indeed," she replied. "If possible, more so. My wheel is a true friend, and I'm sure I would be lost without it."

"Did you see much riding East?" continued the banker.

"More than ever before. The well-paved cities seemed to literally swarm with bicycles, and ladies and gentlemen of every station might be seen spinning here and there on their wheels, some in the pursuit of pleasure, some of business. But whatever the motive, no one can say the riders were not the healthier and happier for their riding. The increase in the bicycle trade has been phenomenal, Mr. Brown. I am informed that some of the large firms are compelled to run day and night in order to fill their orders. In some cities the street car companies are complaining bitterly against the so-called bicycle fad, because the growing custom of riding to and from the office and shop on wheels has cut down their receipts heavily. And the livery men are also complaining. In fact, it is now quite generally admitted that the growth of bicycling has much to do with the low price of horses. Mr. Chauncey Depew recently predicted the practical annihilation of the horse trade."

"But do you not think it is a fad that, like the skating rink craze of a few years ago, will shortly run its course?" I asked.

"Not at all," she replied. "The skating rink had very little to commend it, and much to condemn it. But the wheel has very much to commend it, and practically nothing to condemn it. It is a time-saver, and if one must keep a horse, also a money-saver, for the wheel needs no corn and oats, and no groom. It is a health-giver, as many an overworked professional man and woman can testify. Used to excess, as it has been in a few instances perhaps, the wheel has not been helpful. But on the whole, I do not see how any competent critic can but pronounce the bicycle an epoch-making invention. Zola, the celebrated French author, who, if not the most moral, is one of the most prolific writers of the century, rides a bicycle. In a recent interview he said: 'I ride a bicycle for exercise. I am a great believer in the healthful influence of the bicycle. Within fifty years I believe it will be considered a necessity in every household. All will ride, father, mother, daughters and sons.' If the perpetual candidate for the French Academy should come to New York, which he threatens to do, he would find his prophecy largely fulfilled already."

Her easy, pointed talk charmed me. It was so different from the little nothings I had been in the habit of expecting from society ladies. She was certainly a study, this girl in bloomers. She was jovial, but not silly; well-informed, but not affected; cordial, but not soft. I had always been opposed to bicycling on general principles, especially on the part of ladies. But after this fair-minded and exhaustive deliverance there seemed absolutely nothing to say, and I very properly held my tongue. The plates had just been removed, and the dessert brought in. Dallying over his coffee, Mr. Brown finally startled me from a gentle reverie in which I saw bicycles, street-cars, horses, and fat corporation presidents, by putting our talented guest another question, more startling to me than the first one, and yet more interesting. Again he shot me a merry glance from the corner of his mischievous eye.

"And what have you to say for bloomers, Miss Thorne?"

"Ah, Mr. Brown," she replied, with a most winsome smile, "bloomers are my hobby. It is the most sensible idea in woman's dress that has been advanced in centuries."

"Why do you think so?"

"For several reasons. First, because bloomers do not impede the movement of the wearer like skirts. Any form of dress that impedes in getting about ought to be forever discarded. Just think of women wearing heavy skirts that hang in multitudinous folds about their limbs. It is no wonder they cannot walk, or run, or fence, or ride properly, or do anything that requires action as well as men. But with bloomers, it is as easy for women to climb the hills, or row, or ride a wheel, or wrestle, or jump as her brothers. In the second place, bloomers are more healthful. They are light and airy, and feel good on the wearer, while skirts are a constant drag, drag, drag, and whether supported from the hips or shoulders, they are an intolerable and inexcusable nui-

SHE WAS CERTAINLY A STUDY, THIS GIRL IN
BLOOMERS. SHE WAS JOVIAL, BUT NOT SILLY;
WELL INFORMED, BUT NOT AFFECTED; CORDIAL,
BUT NOT SOFT.—Page 35.

sance, causing or aggravating an innumerable number of diseases peculiar to the gentler sex. It is well known that specialists thrive to-day on diseases of women. Half their receipts would be cut off, were skirts abolished. They are not only disease-producers, but disease-carriers. Trailing the dusts of the street, they gather disease germs and carry them into the home in thousands of instances.

"In the third place, bloomers are less expensive. It takes eight yards or more to make a skirt properly, while one-half the amount will suffice for bloomers. And this is a big item with the million. In the fourth place, bloomers add to a woman's charms. In all ages a woman's form has been the artist's ideal of beauty. If it is true that art is a developer, then it is a sin against art and beauty to completely enshroud woman's lower limbs, which constitute one of her chiefest charms. Bloomers have been called vulgar. If so, then art is vulgar. 'To the pure all things are pure.' It would not be wise to trust very far those who condemn bloomers because they expose the form more perfectly than skirts. No, from every standpoint of consideration, bloomers are better than skirts, and I am glad to believe they have come to stay. Already thousands of our best ladies are wearing them on their wheels and in the gymnasium, while a few have adopted them as their constant habit. It is only a question of time when skirts will be curiosities of the barbarous past."

"Bravo!" exclaimed the banker's wife.

"Well, why don't you wear 'em?" said the banker.

"For the same reason that many others do not, I suppose—Mother Grundy. Few women are so brave and capable as our dear Miss Thorne. Consequently the reform moves too slowly. You remember, Mr. Brown, that when this sweet girl first appeared on the streets of Smithville on her bicycle, the gossips fed upon her in fiendish delight, for she was the first lady in the city to ride. But now hundreds ride, and it is thought quite proper."

"And I am now undergoing a similar experience with my bloomers, Mrs. Brown," said Miss Thorne, laughing, "and the gentlemen can depend upon it that it will end in a similar triumph for the right and sensible. I believe I am so far the only lady in our town to wear bloomers habitually, but this will not be so long. Many of our fair young girls may be seen donned in bloomers of evenings when riding their wheels. By the way, I ran across a nice little editorial in the Boston Standard yesterday which I cut out and put in my portmanteau on purpose for you, Mrs. Brown. I feel sure that you will be delighted with it, and if you will excuse me one moment I will get it and read it to the gentlemen at this stage of the discussion."

Returning, she read as follows:—

"That the ordinary dress worn by women is entirely unsuitable for the bicycle goes without saying. In the attempt to find a garb which will allow the rider the necessary freedom of action, and yet preserve the proprieties, many monstrosities have been produced; but these defective dresses will disappear in the process of time, and good taste will find a way to unite utility and propriety in some general style of garments to which the majority of lady bicyclists will conform.

"Even then some of these public howlers will object to the bicycle for women unless it can be rigged with a side-saddle and its power for health and recreation practically destroyed. We have here a remnant of the old superstition about 'woman's sphere' which ought to have no influence in this day of intelligent and broad-minded consideration of all social and moral questions.

"These antediluvian objectors need to be taught that character is in the individual and not in the dress, and that it is more clearly revealed by manner than by garments. A modest woman will not lose her modesty because she gets out of the corsets and stays, the tight boots and heavy skirts, which have crippled her body and hampered her activity so long, and puts on garments which allow the freedom of action which God intended the human body to have when He put it together.

"The present trend toward open air sports is a hopeful sign. The mingling of the sexes in wholesome exercise will do much to prevent the evils which croaking objectors fear. We need an advance and

not a retreat. When sex ceases to become empha-
sized in dress, the baser passions will have less
stimulus. When men and women forget sex differ-
ences in the common comradeship which is possible
between intellectual and social equals, unless the
whole plan of human life is a bungle, we shall have
less occasion to build a wall around chastity."

"Already the light is breaking. It will not be long
till skirts are relegated to the garret."

"Heaven grant it," said Mrs. Brown, who always
carried piety into her reforms. "When that day
comes, I'll wear bloomers, too."

And the banker roared with laughter. We all returned to the parlor, where the conversation merged
into other subjects, and after a pleasant hour, we
bade each other good-night and retired to our rooms.
When I arose the next morning and appeared at
breakfast, the object of my study had been gone an
hour. She was an early riser, while I was from long
habit a late one. I felt that I had suffered a real loss
in her departure. But Mrs. Brown assured me that
we should see her often, as she considered the distance from Smithville a mere step, and was in the
habit of running out frequently. And she did. One
day she visited us and remained several hours, and
we took a ride on the lake together. We became
well-acquainted, and it was therefore quite natural
that I should receive an invitation to visit her at her
home before my return to the city.

GRACE THORNE AT HOME.

CHAPTER II.

GRACE THORNE AT HOME.

> "Home is the resort
> Of love, of joy, of peace, of plenty; where,
> Supporting and supported, polished friends
> And dear relations mingle into bliss."
> —THOMSON.

My six weeks at the Villa had passed all too quickly. In an ideal spot I had led an ideal life. Hence it was with regret that I began to think of my close quarters in the city, and the hum-drum life that I must lead within its walls. But such is life. Where duty calls the true man will always respond. Six weeks in the bosom of nature had enlarged my manhood, and I felt equal to any task.

It was Thursday afternoon. I was to spend the evening with Miss Thorne at her home, and leave on the following day for the city. As I dressed for the occasion, my thoughts were busy, as they had been more or less for three weeks, studying this new woman whom I was about to visit in her native lairs. She was so different from other women, and yet so like what a woman ought to be. Certainly I was not interested in her more than a mere acknowledgment of this.   And yet, somehow I was sorry that I had to leave her, and fondly hoped that it would not be long till I could see her again.

Still, I was not quite sure that I liked her.   I felt morally certain that her pronounced notions on the new woman question were repulsive to me, and yet I could not tell exactly why.   But I feared I would find her somewhat loud and stern in the home.   Certainly a woman who wore bloomers and attended dress reform conventions could not be otherwise.   I was born and brought up in Kentucky, where woman is almost the idol of the gallant men.   My mother and sisters were representatives of their sex in gentleness and refinement along every standard line. How this fair Wisconsin lass would shock their precious sensibilities! thought I.   And yet why?   In three weeks I had not heard her say nor seen her do a single indelicate thing.   After all, was it not Dame Fashion who ruled opinion, and was not the aristocratic old thing wrong herself?

Mrs. Brown drove me over in her light phaeton and chaperoned me to the very door of the Thorne residence.   Then with kindly apologies she excused herself from accepting Miss Grace's cordial invitation to remain, saying that she had several errands to attend to, and promising to send a carriage for me at 10 o'clock.

The Thorne residence was a plain but roomy old cottage located in the center of a five-acre plot at the

BUT FEARED I WOULD FIND HER SOMEWHAT LOUD
AND STERN IN THE HOME.—Page 46.

edge of town. The grounds were well kept, and abounded in beautiful shade and fruit trees, shrubbery, blue grass lawns, and winding gravel drives. Within were marks of good taste everywhere to be seen. Nothing ostentatious or stiff, but a general air of quiet, sensible refinement. I was ushered into the parlor and shown to an easy chair. Miss Thorne threw open the blinds, gave the lace curtains a little touch or two, and then seated herself on a low divan just opposite me.

"I like the sunshine," said she, pleasantly. "It's good medicine. I never could bear a close room, with no sunshine to brighten its dreary recesses. How have you enjoyed your vacation, Doctor?"

"Very much, indeed," I replied. "Spring Rock Villa is a delightful place, and the Browns are most hospitable and kind. I have gained several pounds in flesh, and acquired a genuine Mexican tan."

"Good!" exclaimed my fair friend, clapping her hands. "How happy and natural it is to be healthful. So many professional people seem to think it incompatible to be well. I trust you may never fall into that error."

"But one cannot always be well?" I questioned.

"Why not? Disease is abnormal. If the human family would live normally there would be little disease. But with our present habits of diet, dress, rest and exercise, little wonder that half the race is sick and the other half complaining. I believe it is

Helen Gilbert Ecob who says, 'It is false civilization which brings the refinements of disease'. And she is right. Especially is this true with reference to my own sex. There is a popular notion that it is natural for woman to be sickly. It is a pernicious fallacy. The term 'weaker vessel' is wrested from its true meaning, and woman is practically prohibited from being strong. It is a sad mistake, Doctor, and it is high time that we were awaking from such unreasonable conclusions. By the way, perhaps you would like to see the library? Then let us step in, and I will call your attention to a quotation or two from some of my 'authorities,' as you ministers say."

And she led the way to the library, a cosy room on the ground floor at the left of the main entrance to the house. As we passed across the hall I observed that my study, as I had begun to call her in my own mind, was still arrayed in bloomers. Not the heavy, velvet ones she had worn on the road, but a garment made out of some light, fluffy material. Her hose were evidently of silk, while a pair of dainty slippers had taken the place of her boots. Her step was as light as a fairy's, and her general air one of ease and contentment. It was refreshing.

"What a pleasant room!" I exclaimed, as we passed into the library.

"Yes, I think so," said she. "I spend many delightful hours here. I like books, and a few flowers in

AND SHE LED THE WAY TO THE LIBRARY, A COZY
ROOM ON THE GROUND FLOOR.—Page 50.

summer, and a glowing grate in winter adds greatly to their charm I think. This is the dearest room about the house to me. Who was it that wrote that little couplet—

"No little room so warm and bright,
Wherein to read, wherein to write?"

Tennyson, I believe. I'm sure you clergymen can appreciate the sentiment, for you are men of culture. Have this chair. Now let me see: I wanted to cite you to a remark of Prof. Cowperthwait's on this woman question in which you have shown so much interest. He says: 'The fact that the female is physically inferior to the male is not due so much to her natural organization as to the fact that the mode of life which modern society forces upon her is unnatural, and begets physical degeneration. It is only when the deteriorating influence of refined society begins to operate that we find the physical organization of the female depreciating, and her powers of endurance, as well as her capacity of resisting disease, becoming inferior to those of the male'. Instead of 'refined society' I would have said what is called refined society. A truly conducted society would give to woman those equal advantages with man which must be allowed before she can be as strong. Dr. Kellogg is right when he says: 'I can see no reason why a well-developed woman may not equal in endurance a man of the same size and development.' The great trouble to-day is that most women seem to regard themselves as 'pre-ordained to hysterics, tears, and nervous prostration'. She rarely attempts any exercise or work that involves an honest outlay of muscle, and hence she remains comparatively feeble and subject to all sorts of physical ailments. I believe in a thorough-going equality of the sexes, Doctor, and the world will never be what it is capable of being and ought to be till we have it."

"But, Miss Thorne, is there not a serious danger that woman will become masculanized?" said I.

"No more than that men will become femininized," said she, earnestly. "This idea that the new woman must necessarily be masculine is all talk, and emanates from disorganized brains I fear. And yet I grant you that some silly girls have given cause for complaint by their ridiculous imitation of man's dress, the wearing of vests, starched shirt fronts, male neck-ties, derby hats, etc. Such creatures are not representatives of the new womanhood for which we are praying, but rather the caricature of it. It is unfair to those of us who are pleading for a genuine, all-around womanhood to hold up these gum-chewing, giggling, man-aping specimens of a depraved fad as the outcome of our efforts. And it is unjust to blame all equal rights advocates for the presence in the world now and then of an iron-willed, coarse, rule-or-ruin-spirited woman. There have always been chicken-hearted men, and there will al-

YOU MUST KNOW THAT THE NEW WOMAN RIDES
A STRADDLE.—Page 57.

ways be donkey-hearted women I suppose; but both are excrescences, and should not be taken as representatives.—But come, Doctor, let us take a stroll through the garden."

"With pleasure," said I.

She donned a light summer hat, and gaily led the way. We wandered aimlessly among the trees and flowers, now stopping to examine some choice shrub, or to enjoy the fragrance of some favorite blossom. Meanwhile my lady talked fluently, never tiring. And I was amazed at her knowledge of botany. She knew the name of every plant, and could analyze with the skill of a professor. Upon reaching the stables in the course of our saunterings, I was again surprised to see my study enter the stalls and pet the horses. She knew each animal by name, and patted their respective necks and stroked their manes with the delight of a child.

"Do you ride horse-back, Miss Thorne?" I asked.

"Oh, certainly," said she. "But not upon the customary side-saddle. It may shock you, Doctor, but you must know that the new woman rides a-straddle. I use a common saddle, and can manage a horse as well as the most dexterous cow-boy, I fancy."

"A-straddle!" I exclaimed, and I felt almost like apologizing for using such indelicate words. "Why, Miss Thorne?"

"Because it's sensible. Why should a woman ride otherwise? It's barbarous—no, it is worse than that,

for barbarous women do not ride sideways. I do not
know who invented such a custom, but it certainly
has no place in this enlightened age. But it's a
necessary accompaniment of skirts. Side saddles
are both ugly and dangerous, but they are a necessity so long as women wear skirts. With bloomers
one can ride in the only natural and sensible way, a-
straddle. I have been riding so two years or more.
At first the neighbors were dazed, and hopelessly inquired of each other, What will that girl do next?
But they gradually became accustomed to it, other
ladies joined the procession, and now it is quite common in Smithville to see ladies riding a-straddle. It
is strange to me, Doctor, that so progressive a people
as Americans should tolerate so many heathenish
customs."

"Yes, very strange," said I, for I did not know what
else to say.

Returning toward the house, we came to a large
open space, surrounded by rustic seats and great
shade trees.

"Ah, here's our exercise grounds," explained Miss
Thorne in answer to my questioning look. "Sister
and I spend an hour here each day. We used to have
rare sport here together before brother married and
moved to the city. He was very muscular—a splendid athlete. And yet, Doctor, I beg leave to inform
you that he could excel me in very few feats."

And by way of illustration she picked up a pole

AND BY WAY OF ILLUSTRATION, SHE PICKED UP A
POLE AND VAULTED.—Page 58.

and vaulted fully eight feet. And then she put the
iron shot a phenomenally long distance. Gathering
up a heavy pair of dumb-bells she twirled them a few
times about her head, and then, scratching a mark
with the toe of her slipper, jumped farther than I
could have done to save my life, and when in college
I had prided myself somewhat in this art. She ban-
tered me for a foot race, but I blushingly protested,
urging that I had no reputation as a sprinter.

"But I see you have a fine tennis court," said I.
"Suppose we try our hands at a game of tennis?"

"Agreed!"

But she beat me badly.

At last we found ourselves in the parlor again, and
although my study seemed as fresh and sprightly as
when we started on our jaunt, I felt quite weary, and
glad of an opportunity to rest. Perhaps the many
surprises of the hour had had as much to do with
fatiguing me as the exercise; I shall not say. But
at any rate the easy chair felt good, and I remembered
that I had an appetite.

"Now, Doctor, you will excuse me please," said my
gifted entertainer, as she handed me a late magazine.
"I must go and help about dinner."

And before I could recover my senses she had gone
like a flash of sunshine. The room actually seemed
dark, and I wondered whether my fair enchantress
were not a hypnotist. Help about the dinner? Is
that a part of the code of this new womanhood?

thought I. Well, if so, all hail! For it is an axiom that the nearest route to man's heart is through his stomach, and it is a well known fact that the average domestic never reaches the heart in that way.

Promptly at seven dinner was announced. Mr. Thorne had left his store at six. I was favorably impressed with both himself and his sweet-faced companion. Mrs. Thorne was fifty, I judged, and as perfect a specimen of well-rounded womanhood as one often meets. The younger daughter, Miss Josephine, was a close imitation of her sister, though not so mature and self-poised. It was an interesting family, and the dinner hour was pleasantly spent.

"Will you have another piece of cake?" said Miss Grace, just as we were concluding the sixth and last course.

"Upon one consideration," said I.

"What is it?"

"That you inform me who made it."

"With pleasure. I did."

I expected her to apologize, and say that it was not as good as she had hoped. But she did nothing of the kind. She was the most unusual girl I had ever met.

"You probably observed that our menu was very plain, Doctor," continued Miss Grace. "We are all enthusiasts over plain, wholesome food. We are particular as to what we eat, and as to how it is cooked. The quantity is a minor consideration. Papa does

PROMPTLY AT SEVEN DINNER WAS SERVED.—
Page 62.

all the marketing, and he will pardon me for saying in his presence that he is a wise and careful purchaser. He buys nothing simply because it is cheap. And when it comes to the preparation of what he buys for the table, I guess that mamma, sister and I are about equally matched in ability. Sometimes one oversees the cooking, and sometimes another. We never trust Bridget alone. Cookery is a fine art, and we think should be studied as such. Poor cookery is a very prolific cause of disease."

"And divorce," added Mr. Thorne. "Sad biscuits have caused many a sad home. I am proud to say that my daughters are both excellent cooks, Doctor. Their mother trained them religiously in the art, and whether it falls to their lot to bake a cake or turn a steak, they can do it as nicely as any chef. And then they have studied dietetics. I am a firm believer in the theory that we can make or unmake disease by the food we eat. For instance, when I was a boy I used to eat pork and buckwheat all winter. The result was thick blood and boils in the spring. Now I eat no pork, and, in fact, very little meat of any kind. While not strictly a vegetarian, I am very partial to cereals. We eat plentifully of fruit, nuts and vegetables. Hence wife and I have passed the 'dead line of fifty' in the primest of health, and, barring accidents, we fully expect to cover another half century each before we depart this life."

"All you say sounds reasonable," said I. "But I

confess that I have never given these questions much attention."

"But pardon me, Doctor, you should do so," continued the old gentleman pleasantly. "Ministers, as a rule, are the hardest worked of any professional class, and perhaps oftenest break down in health. I have been long persuaded that it is not work that kills so much as improper habits of life. Poorly selected and still more poorly cooked food, irregular hours, worry—here lies the cause of the majority of break-downs. There are about 350 colleges in this country. Could I have my way I should establish a school of cookery in connection with each, and then, rich or poor, high or low, every student should be compelled to give this grave subject due consideration. Had I a dozen daughters, I should feel that their education was incomplete till every one had learned to do well everything in the kitchen, from scrubbing the floor to making a bridal cake."

"I am very much interested in what you say, Mr. Thorne," I replied, "and I promise you that I will think seriously on this subject. There is undoubtedly more in it than the average student imagines."

Dinner over, we all repaired to the parlor. I observed that the younger of the daughters also wore bloomers like her sister. And she was almost as attractive. My antipathy was fast fading away, and I began to feel more bold in discussing the theme. Mrs. Thorne did not wear bloomers. I wondered why, and so inquired, somewhat shyly:

A STYLE OF DRESS CONSIDERED QUITE PROPER
THESE DAYS.—Page 69.

"You have not abandoned the custom of our mothers with references to skirts, I see, Mrs. Thorne."

"No, but I should be only too glad to do so. Mrs. Brown and I have often considered the matter, but as yet we have been too timid to dare it. I trust the day is not far distant when women can dress sensibly without exciting comment."

"By the way, Doctor," said Miss Grace, "I presume you remember how the lords of Chicago not long ago ruled that a lady in bloomers was a proper subject for arrest if seen on the streets of that pure-eyed city? What a travesty on justice! But the world is advancing. Only a few years ago a lady was arrested in a Western city for wearing a 'Mother Hubbard,' now a style of dress that is considered quite proper. It is only a question of time when we will emerge from the dark ages on this subject of dress, and then the world will be better."

"All of which is very good and true," remarked Mr. Thorne. "But perhaps the Doctor would enjoy a little music, daughters?"

"Most assuredly," said I.

And without the customary begging, the young ladies stepped to the piano. Miss Grace acted as accompanist and also took the soprano part in a clear, rich voice, while Miss Josephine sang the alto and turned the leaves. Several duets were rendered most charmingly, and then Miss Grace played some from Beethoven and Liszt. I had heard great performers,

but none who so enlisted my sympathies. She played
without affectation, as she did everything else, but
with a soul-power and faultlessness of technique that
astonished me. Here was a girl that seemed to be
equally at home in the library, the lawn, the kitchen
and the parlor. And she was no novice. Few could
equal her in whatever she undertook. This was delightful, and I secretly prayed, oh, Lord, give this
poor old world more like her, bloomers and all!

Arising from the instrument, she tarried awhile
at her father's side, throwing her pretty arm around
his neck and gently toying with his curly gray locks
as only a loving daughter can toy, and presently resumed her place on the low divan where she had first
sat upon my arrival. As she caressed her father,
something said to me, Wouldn't it be nice if you were
her father? But I stifled the thought. For shame!
said my better conscience. You are not worthy to be
such a girl's father. And I'm quite sure I wasn't.

Another hour of pleasant conversation, in which
books, music, fashion, politics, and a little of everything played a part, in all of which I found that my
study was admirably posted, and I took my departure, with the kindest of invitations to return if ever
convenient to do so. Burying myself in the cushions
of the carriage, I dreamed with my eyes open all the
way to the villa, concluding with the mental ejacula-
tion as I reached the gate:

"Well, I'll see more of you, heaven willing."

A QUARREL
WITH MOTHER GRUNDY.

CHAPTER III.

A QUARREL WITH MOTHER GRUNDY.

"I'll be at charge for a looking-glass;
  And entertain a score or two of tailors,
  To study fashions to adorn my body.
  Since I am crept in favor with myself,
  I will maintain it with some little cost."
                                —RICHARD III.

"Back again!"

"Back again, my good brother," said I.

It was my sexton, and we were right glad to see each other. The sexton of a church is usually supposed to be a man of bad heart, shiftless manners and worthless soul. But in my parish it was not so. Uncle John was a good, hard-working, painstaking, wide-awake old Scotchman. He had seen better days in the highlands, but through a chain of circumstances over which he had had no control, he had been reduced to poverty, and in his old age was compelled to earn his daily bread at manual toil.

"And how has everything gone?" said L.

"Just fairly wael, dominie," said he.

The old man always called me "dominie." But I freely forgave him little eccentricities like that, for among all my friends I had none more valuable nor more true.

"Well, Uncle, tell me all about it," said I.

And in his quaint, old dialect he rehearsed the doings of the people during my absence, collectively and individually, so far as he knew, and what he didn't know was hardly worth knowing, I suppose. Like any flock in the absence of its shepherd, they had scattered somewhat and some of them had gotten into mischief. But our large auditorium was soon filled again, and the work took on its old-time enthusiasm. My outing had given tone to every power, and my heavy duties now seemed light.

Winter came, and with it an endless round of receptions, balls, dinners, theater parties and other popular pitfalls for the tender saint. Many of my members moved in aristocratic circles, and I had always imagined that it must be quite proper to do so if one had the capital and inclination. Personally, I seldom went out, except to my various church gatherings, and so knew very little of society. Occasionally I spent the evening with the Browns, who had returned from their villa early in October, and who cared as little as myself for the doings of the "four hundred."

But at last I became aroused. A spiritual pall seemed to be hanging over my people. While the services were elegant, there were few conversions. And for the first time in my ministry I noticed that

THERE WERE APPARENTLY NO POOR, BUT ONLY
THE RICH AND REFINED.—Page 77.

among the crowds that came to worship with us there were apparently no poor, but only the rich and refined. So one day I concluded to "go slumming" and see if I could learn what was the matter. It had become very popular for preachers to visit the sore spots of our metropolis, and then deliver sensational sermons on the subject. But I did not go with any such an idea. I merely wanted to see and learn what I could with a view to solving the problem of non-church attendance on the part of the poor who were in easy walking distance of my church. Clad in a business suit, I visited the home of many poverty-stricken and degraded people.

"Why do you not attend church?" I asked again and again, now of some horny-handed laborer, and then of some tired children and dirt-bedraggled mother.

"What has the church done for us?" was the invariable answer. "Rich people can go to church, but it is no place for us poor devils."

"I am sure you do the church an injustice," I would argue. "My people would be delighted to see the pews filled with the poor at every service."

"Don't you believe it, parson," said an old washer-woman. "They may talk that way in prayer meetin' sometimes, but if I should go there with my four children some bright Sunday, their looks would freeze us out. No, no. Religion is all right, I reckon, but church folks is awful stuck up nowadays. They needn't be, though, for I've seen enough with these old eyes of mine to know that some as live in big houses on the boulevard is no nearer heaven than us poor trash as has to work for a livin'."

It was no use to parley. After several excursions among the homes of the lower classes, some by day and some by night, I returned to my study with a heavy heart. There seemed to be an invulnerable prejudice among the poor of all classes against the rich and their churches. Mine was no exception I learned from authentic sources. I found that in Chicago, as in England, the "submerged tenth" were low-browed, low-spirited, and low-lived. And yet the remark of the old washer-woman, that her despised class were as near heaven as many of the upper tendom, compelled me to think. At first I did not believe it. But in order to satisfy myself thoroughly, I concluded to inaugurate a series of investigations. I entered society with all the alacrity of a debutante. Having numerous friends that were on the top wave, I found no difficulty in getting into the swim.

Six weeks' experience and observation convinced me that the laundress was right. Beneath the glare and glitter of gilded society, I had detected sepulchers of moral filth that astonished me beyond measure. Much against my will I had become convinced that hundreds of both sexes who move in the so-called best society, and stood high in church circles, were morally rotten to the core. Vanity, vanity, van-

BENEATH THE GLARE AND GLITTER OF GILDED SO-
CIETY, I HAD DETECTED SEPULCHERS OF MORAL
FILTH THAT ASTONISHED ME BEYOND MEASURE.
Page 78.

ity! thought I. Truly King Solomon was a wise scribe. I could hold my tongue no longer. So, on the first Sunday in Lent, 1896, I delivered a sermon that seriously offended Mother Grundy, and the old dame at once set a thousand tongues a-wagging. Among other things, I said:

"Beloved, my mind has been greatly exercised for some months over certain conditions which seem to threaten the welfare of the church. We have no poor people in our services. Upon visiting among them for days, I discovered a deep and bitter prejudice existing against the church because of its lack of sympathy with the lower classes, and because of its worldliness. It was argued that my people were no nearer heaven than those who made no pretensions. Accordingly I threw off clerical conservatism for a time and entered society. I attended all sorts of bon-ton gatherings, and studiously examined every thread in your social fabric. The result is a burdened heart. Although dressed in soft garments like those who sit in kings' houses, and protected by the silken cords of elite society, there are hypocrites of the worst tpye before me to-day. You have been often here, joining in our songs and partaking of the holy sacrament. But, like Bishop Burrows of London, I have not dared till now to say a word that might offend you. And as he said to his people, so I must say to you, 'there are ladies whose faces I see here to-day with whom no decent tradesman's wife or daughter would associate.' You would never suspect it, but I have seen some of your society belles smoking opium in infamous, but gilded dives. I have listened to your insipid conversation, and watched your sensual flirtations till my nerves were benumbed. I have studied every phase of the dance question, carefully witnessing the outcome all the way from parlor quadrilles to ball-room waltzes, and I am compelled to say that I solemnly believe the testimony of numerous hack drivers that this popular but devilish amusement has made many a private carriage a bed on wheels, and many a wealthy home a house of easy morals!

"Sometime ago I delivered a prelude on 'fads that will become permanent customs,' you will remember. On that occasion I advocated the wearing of bloomers. Some of you precious matrons and heavenly damsels affected to be shocked. You said that your pastor should be ashamed to espouse the cause of so vulgar a fashion. And yet I have seen you self-same critics in decolette costumes in the ball-room, shamefully exposing your nakedness—sporting a dress a hundred times more vulgar than the harmless and sensible bloomers you so strenuously oppose.

"Oh, my dear people! Your whole course is wrong, frightfully wrong. Society as at present conducted is making libertines of our men, and polished profligates of our women. It is dwarfing both soul and body. It develops a useless class of novel-reading, ease-taking, money-spending, virtue-breaking, health-

I HAVE SEEN SOME OF YOUR SOCIETY BELLES
SMOKING OPIUM IN INFAMOUS, BUT GILDED
DIVES.—Page 82.

wrecking, gnat-straining imitations of a true manhood and womanhood. Out upon it! As for me, I
would turn from the past and call you to repentance.
Let us clean up, and present a better picture to a lost
and ruined world. There are a thousand better ways
in which to spend our time, strength and money than
in the idiotic whirl of a depraved and hell-besmirched
society. Let us enlarge our house, make all seats
free, and then go out into the highways and hedges
and compel the poor, the maimed, the halt, and the
blind to come in. Man's greatest mission is to serve.
To bear a cup of cold water to one of God's little ones
is better than to take a city. What seems right in society, religion, politics and everywhere is often
wrong; and what seems wrong is often right. The
Word of God is our only infallible guide. Remember-
ing this, may we set ourselves in order and enter upon
a season of real progress along every private and
public line."

The effect of this deliverance was like that of a
cyclone let loose in the congregation. Some arose
and left the building in disgust. Others frowned
and bit their lips. A few nodded approval. Among
the last named were Banker Brown and his good
wife, than whom I had no truer friends. The sermon was published in full in several of the daily
papers, and forthwith precipitated a storm. All
classes discussed the matter, and the news of the
commotion soon spread from ocean to ocean. With-

out intending to be sensational, I had innocently provoked the greatest sensation of the season. Many
condemned me and my utterances in the most violent
terms, while a goodly number expressed their agree-
ment. At any rate, a revival spirit was quickened
in many churches all over the land, a general self-
examination was begun, and thousands were made
better men and women, I trust.

In my own church the effect promised to be disas-
trous at first. A large and influential element
promptly insisted on my resignation. But a majority
of the officiary were opposed to my leaving. Under
ordinary circumstances, I should have stepped down
and out very quickly. But as it was, I felt it to be my
duty to remain, which I did. More than 100 of my
flock called for letters of dismissal, however, and thus
was inaugurated a revival in the church which continued for many weeks, and resulted in a mighty in-
gathering, scores coming from among the laboring
classes, as well as from the higher walks of life. The
spiritual life of the congregation was revolutionized,
and the usefulness of the church multiplied many
fold.

While the excitement over my sermon was at its
highest, I was surprised one morning on opening my
mail to find a letter post-marked "Smithville." It
was addressed in a bold, running hand, and at first I
could not imagine from whom it could have come.
Breaking the seal, I read as follows:

SPORTING A DRESS A HUNDRED TIMES MORE VUL-
GAR THAN THE HARMLESS AND SENSIBLE BLOOM-
ERS YOU SO STRENUOUSLY OPPOSE.—Page 82.

Smithville, Wis., March 1, 1896.

Rev. Dr. Frank Charlton, Chicago, Ill.

Dear Sir—Having read your sermon as published in the daily papers, I hasten to congratulate you on the stand you have taken for the right. Do not flinch. Criticisms will be hurled upon you from every source, but remember that the price of progress is that bravery which dares to defend principle. Hold your ground like the true man that I believe you to be, and you will never lack for honorable and capable friends and supporters in your fight against the evils of this corrupt decade. Believe me to be

Sincerely,

GRACE THORNE.

To say that I was pleased is but lightly to express it. I was intoxicated with delight. Although I had not seen Miss Thorne since that pleasant September evening spent at her home, I had by no means forgotten her. Not a line had passed between us. And yet she had grown to be more and more to my life every day. But she seemed inapproachable. I never could bring myself to dare to write her. Now that the ice was broken, I gladly began a most pleasant and profitable correspondence with this remarkable woman. With each letter I was more and more impressed with her originality and maturity of thought, her unfeigned sincerity and her tremendous earnestness.

"What do you think of Miss Thorne by this time?" said Mrs. Brown abruptly one evening as I was dining at the banker's hospitable home.

"Why do you ask?" said I, somewhat puzzled.

"Because I admire her very much myself, and am anxious that others shall, especially my pastor, with whom, she inadvertently informed me, she is corresponding," said Mrs. Brown. "She is a magnificent specimen of the new woman, Doctor, and I only hope her letters delight you as they do me. Among all my correspondents I have none for whose letters I look so anxiously."

"Ditto, Mrs. Brown," said I. "My correspondence with Miss Thorne has been delightful, indeed, to me, and I can truly say that I admire her very much. As you know, I have long since lost my antipathy for bloomers, consequently there is nothing to prevent us being the best of friends."

"You will pardon me, Doctor," said Mrs. Brown, earnestly, "but I wish to say to you frankly that I should be gratified beyond expression to see you more than friends. I would not pose as a match-maker, for I believe that all true unions are planned in heaven; but I would simply suggest the matter to you, and urge that what you do be done quickly."

"Why this haste, Mrs. Brown?" said I.

"Because you need just such a helper in your great work as Miss Grace would be. A man's only half equipped for life's battle till he's married. And then she is just at that age when it is perilous for one to move slowly if he would win her."

"But, Mrs, Brown, I am not sure that I wish to marry. And if I were, I am not sure that Miss Thorne would be my choice. She is an admirable lady—in fact, I know of none for whom I entertain greater respect. But just at present I am so deeply absorbed with my work that I fear I would make her a poor husband even if she could be induced to have me. However, I will think about it," said I, laughingly.

"Well, think fast and hard," said the banker's wife. "She has many suitors."

That night I retired late. The conversation with Mrs. Brown had precipitated new and strange thoughts in my mind. After all, she was right. I did need a helper. Miss Thorne was certainly well qualified to fill the bill. She was now at the age when most girls of her station marry. She had many suitors. All these things passed and repassed through my brain as I meditated before a glowing grate.

But she was so pronounced in her views and habits. What would my friends say? Ah! Mother Grundy, that matters little. I've had one tilt with you, and I'm ready for another if necessary.

She has many suitors. Well, what of it! She is under no obligations to me, nor I to her. And yet, I don't like it. Many suitors! Well, we will see about that.

And I turned to my desk and wrote as follows:

Chicago, April 15, 1896.

Miss Grace Thorne, Smithville, Wis.

Esteemed Friend—Your last kind letter was received three days ago. As usual, its perusal afforded me much pleasure. Concerning your questions, relative to the various reform movements with which I am humbly identified, I would respectfully waive an answer until I can see you personally. Am sure I can make the subject much more interesting and profitable to you in this way than by writing any number of pages.

Feeling somewhat overworked, anyhow, I am confident a few days in the country would be of benefit to me. My friend Brown is going out to his villa next week to make preliminary arrangements for the annual outing, and has asked me to run out with him. If it would suit your convenience and pleasure for me to spend an afternoon and evening at your home again, I will come. The memory of my former visit, and your kind hospitality, makes me bold to solicit a similar experience.

Please remember me to your parents and sister, and favor me with an immediate reply.

Respectfully Yours,

FRANK CHARLTON.

It was a very simple affair, but, contrary to all my experience in letter writing, I was compelled to rewrite it three times, and must have read it over a dozen. When I had finished the task, my fire had gone out and the room was growing cool. I put on my great coat and went out to the corner mail box. The stars were peeping down from every quarter of the sky. Save the monotonous foot-falls of a sleepy policeman who was doing his beat, everything was still. I returned to my room and was soon dreaming of blue eyes and bloomers.

AN AFFAIR OF THE HEART.

CHAPTER IV.

AN AFFAIR OF THE HEART.

"Something the heart must have to cherish,
  Must love, and joy, and sorrow learn;
Something with passion clasp, or perish,
  And in itself to ashes burn."
                                    —LONGFELLOW.

Of course, the reply was quick and favorable. A most hearty invitation was extended, and I began preparations at once for the trip. While down town doing a little shopping, I ran into the bank and was shown to Mr. Brown's private office.

"I'm here to say that your invitation is accepted, Mr. Brown," said I. "After some consideration, I've concluded to go. I'm a little jaded from the heavy duties of the past few months, and a few days at the villa will do me good."

"Right, sir!" said the banker in his hearty manner. "I'm glad you have decided to accompany me. We'll take our guns, for duck hunting is not bad up there just now. We'll start to-morrow evening."

It was a pleasant ride. The fields were robed in green and the trees were leaving. Orchards were in blossom, and the wild flowers were beginning to peep out here and there along the roadway. The meadow

lark was in his glory and seemed to be wishing me a
hearty god-speed.

The old butler at the villa had been apprised of the
hour of our arrival, and his good wife had prepared a
tempting dinner. We retired early after the repast,
and arose with the sun the following morning. Having kept the real secret of my trip in my own heart, I
was cautious not to do or say anything that would ex-
cite the banker's suspicions. So, although I was
very anxious to visit the Thornes, I put it off the first
day and went gunning with Mr. Brown. We had some
rare sport, bagging a goodly number of fowls. It
was almost night when we returned from our day's
tramp through the marshes. The air was quite raw,
as a stiff wind had been blowing all day. A bright
fire had been kindled in the sitting room, and we
were soon toasting our chilled limbs.

"By the way, Mr. Brown," said I, as we waited the
ringing of the dinner bell and discussed the day's
hunt, "I must run over to Smithville while here and
see the Thornes."

"Better go to-morrow, then," said the banker. "I
will be obliged to look after some affairs about the
place to-morrow. So do your visiting while I attend
to business, and then we'll hunt the next day. If you
wish to send word over, I'll call the boy?"

"If you please," said I.

I hurried to my room and penned a brief message,
which the errand boy crumpled into his pocket as he

mounted a spirited pony and hastened on his journey.

"He's afraid of spooks," explained the old butler as he drew the blinds and proceeded to light the lamps. "He'll be back in no time, for he wouldn't cross Myers' bridge after nine o'clock for all the money in the county."

"What's the matter with the bridge?" I inquired.

"Oh, nothin', I guess," said the old servant. "But the old settlers tell as how a man named Myers used to live in that old cabin on t'other side of the creek, and collect toll in the early days before the crossing was free. One dark night he went out to let some travelers over and never showed up again. Everybody said it was foul play. It was supposed that he was murdered, and his body dumped into the stream, although it was never found. Howsumever, they do say that his ghost may be seen any night at nine o'clock walking back and forth on the bridge. Nobody in these parts ever tries to go 'cross at that time. By ten he is gone, and there's no danger. Jim will be back afore nine, you can be sure 'o that."

"Ah, Jerry, you are an old goose to believe in such tales," said Mr. Brown, laughingly. "What's the matter with Aunt Martha to-night? I'm as hungry as a wolf."

Just that minute dinner was called and we sat down to a bountiful spread, in which some of our own game, bagged during the day, figured very prominently. The ducks were done to a turn, and we ate like wood-choppers. After dinner the banker smoked and I played several games of checkers with Jim, who had returned all right, and who said he had delivered the message to the very lady herself.

"Golly, but don't she wear a funny rig, though!" said the boy, as he drove his first man into my king row.

"She still wears bloomers, does she?" said I, not knowing just how to answer him, and feeling inwardly provoked that the young scoundrel should have beheld my lady at all with those big, watery eyes of his.

"Don't know what you call 'em, parson," said he, "but they're the all-firedst odd lookin' things I ever see. I reckon they're mighty nice to get around in though," and he jumped three of my men, and compelled me to crown him another king.

The sun had been up an hour next morning when I arose. Mr. Brown had eaten early, and given orders not to awake me. He had gone out to the fields to give his men some directions. So I ate my breakfast alone, and after a short stroll through the garden found an easy chair on the veranda, where I seated myself and read till noon. We lunched together at one, and by two I was on my way to Smithville. Jim took me over in the phaeton and promised to call for me at eleven o'clock sharp. I knew it was useless to ask him to call at ten, for that would necessitate his crossing Myers' bridge at a bad time. Besides, I

MYERS' BRIDGE.—Page 100.

imagined that it would be very pleasant to stay at the Thornes' till eleven.

"Good afternoon, Doctor," said Miss Thorne.

"Good afternoon," said I. "Of course I find you well."

"Certainly, for it is natural to be well, and I always try to live naturally," said she, gaily. "But you—why, Doctor, I'm surprised to see you looking so thin. The winter's work has evidently been too heavy upon you. Or, perhaps, it is lack of exercise and a proper hygiene."

"It is the latter, I expect," said I. "For I have not worked any harder than usual."

"You don't mean to say that you have neglected a proper care of the body?" said she. "And yet I know you have, for not one professional man in a thousand gives a reasonable degree of attention to the laws of health. But come in, and take this easy chair. I'll call mamma and sister. Papa, of course, it at the store."

The same easy chair! The same low divan, just across the room—I was sure she would sit on it again when she entered! The same cordial manner! It began to seem like home.

Mrs. Thorne and Josephine entered and greeted me almost as warmly as though I had been a friend of long standing. It was all very pleasant. After a half hour's conversation Miss Josephine excused herself in order to keep an engagement down town, and Mrs. Thorne also withdrew, saying that she had promised to call upon a sick lady at four. I was very glad of the younger sister's engagement, and for once was not sorry that somebody was sick. It gave me a better opportunity to enjoy my study.

"What a perfect day!" said Miss Grace, after we had conversed another half hour. "Shall we not take a stroll? or, if you prefer, a spin on the wheel? Papa left his at home on purpose, thinking you might wish to take a ride with me."

"I'm very sorry to say that I have not yet learned, Miss Thorne," said I. "Really, I haven't had leisure since the weather has been nice. Of course, you know the winter is very severe in Chicago, and it was no time to learn the art of cycling."

"But you should have learned last fall. However, I will forgive you this time, and hope for the best. But take a friend's advice and get yourself a wheel before another fortnight passes. It will add strength to those muscles and blood to those cheeks," said she, scanning me with the quick eye of a physician.

"I will take your prescription," said I, "and that just as soon as I return to the city. In the mean-time, I should be glad to take a stroll with so excellent a guide as yourself. I am a good walker, and if I cannot ride with you it is possible that I can tire you out in this old-fashioned way of exercising."

"Don't be too sure of that," said she, laughingly. "I am a good walker, although I consider it an infer-

ior mode of exercise. It is infinitely better than carriage riding, but not so good as horseback riding,
cycling or swimming. But let's be off."

She had been sitting on the low divan, dressed as
always in bloomers. The winter had dealt kindly
with her, I judged, for she seemed fully ten pounds
heavier than in the fall. Her cheeks were pinker,
her shoulders squarer, her shapely limbs plumper.
What a model! thought I. She would make an artist
rave with madness! And yet I'm sure all the money
in the Bank of England couldn't induce her to sit,
for she is innocence personified, beauty inapproachable, an angel in the flesh. Tripping lightly upstairs,
she speedily returned arrayed in walking hat and
shoes. She wore no gloves nor veil. The latter she
explained was injurious to the eyes, slovenly in appearance, and heathenish generally. Gloves would
do for ladies of delicate health, but for her they were
irksome. She was very pronounced.

It was a perfect day. Not cold, nor hot, but just
right. A bright sun, exhilarating atmosphere, blue
sky, green fields, good roads. Is it only the effect
of spring, or is my acquaintance with this lady in
bloomers becoming an affair of the heart? thought I,
as we passed through the stile into the lane which
led toward the woodland, a half mile distant.

"This is a good day for poets," said Miss Thorne.
"Do you like poetry? I do on certain occasions.
This seems to me an appropriate time to quote Whit-

tier, the poet of sunshine and love. I recall one
stanza in his Mogg Megone:

> "'Tis spring-time on the eastern hills!
>   Like torrents gush the summer rills;
>   Through winter's moss and dry dead leaves
>   The bladed grass revives and lives,
>   Pushes the mouldering waste away,
>   And glimpses to the April day."

Some poetry is far-fetched; but this can never be
said of our own Whittier, do you think?"

"Not at all," said I. "That is a pretty thing you
quoted, and it was beautifully done besides. Allow
me to give you four lines from the Italian, which I
think will go well with it:

> "Youth of the year! celestial spring!
>   Again descend thy silent showers;
>   New loves, new pleasures dost thou bring,
>   And earth again looks gay with flowers."

I cannot blame the poetically inclined for being
especially prolific with their verses at this season."

"Nor I," she replied. "Spring has always been my
favorite time of the year. The opening of new life on
every hand is inspiring. It makes one long to be and
to do. Did you ever read that exquisite composition
of Thomas J. Ouseley's entitled 'The Seasons of
Life?' I cannot quote much of it, but think I remember one stanza:

"The soft green grass is growing,
　　O'er meadow and o'er dale;
The silvery founts are flowing
　　Upon the verdant vale;
The pale snowdrop is springing,
　　To greet the glowing sun;
The primrose sweet is flinging
　　Perfume the fields among;
The trees are in the blossom,
　　The birds are in their song,
As spring upon the bosom
　　Of Nature's borne along."

But here we are at the creek. Perhaps we had better dismiss the poets and do our best to appreciate Nature as we see her here face to face. What a beautiful landscape! At least I think so, don't you, Doctor? A thousand times I've been charmed with the view presented from this little rustic bridge."

We had reached a small stream which wound its way along the foot of the hill we had just descended, now darting into the woodland for a few hundred feet, and then shooting across the meadow. Cattle might be seen grazing lazily on either bank, and a flock of sheep were industriously nipping the tender grass on yonder hillside. Here and there could be seen a pretty farm house, invariably painted white, with green window blinds. Most of the barns, which were usually large, were painted red. The contrast of colors as they appeared against a background of living green, was something not soon to be forgotten, and I honestly agreed with my friend that the view was delightful. We stood for some time upon the little rustic bridge, watching the waters play in the sunlight beneath. It was a pebbly place, and a school of little sunfish seemed to be playing hide-and-seek among the larger rocks.

"Play on little fellows while you may," said Miss Thorne. "It will not be long until some boy from the cruel town will espy you, and with baited hook allure you to your fate."

She spoke earnestly, but with a far-away look in her eyes which seemed to see other things than the little fish. I made no reply, and for a time we were silent. Finally she turned those great, searching orbs full upon me and said:

"Doctor, amidst all our joys and sorrows; amidst all our successes and failures; amidst all the sunshine and cloud with which every life is encompassed, is there any such thing as contentment?"

"You have asked me a hard question," said I. "You may remember that the Good Book says 'whatsoever state we are in, therewith to be content;' but I confess that I have always found it a difficult commandment to obey. Phillips Brooks once said that 'the ideal life, the life full of completions, haunts us all. We feel the thing we ought to be beating beneath the thing we are.' This is true in my own case. How have you found it?"

"Precisely the same," said she. "I am a little use-

HERE WE SAT DOWN UNDER A GREAT TREE.—
Page 112.

ful, I guess, but long to be more so. I am happy, but long for still greater happiness. There is so much to do in this wide and wicked world, and time and the tides wait for no man. There are numerous reforms that must be brought about ere this decade close, or our country will cross the threshold of the twentieth century sadly manacled."

We walked on, following a well-beaten path which pushed its way circuitously into the depths of the forest. The farther we went, the taller grew the trees. At last we came to a rugged hill which rose quite abruptly from the level to a height of a hundred feet or more. Miss Thorne insisted on climbing it, which we did, much to my grief, as I had two or three falls in the ascent, tore my trousers and scratched my face. Miss Thorne laughed heartily at my expense. She not only made the trip unscathed, but kindly offered me her hand. Of course, I politely refused any assistance, and clambered up the best way I could. When we reached the summit I was almost out of breath, while she seemed not at all fatigued. Her cheeks were just a little rosier, that was all. And I said to myself, Oh, you magnificent new woman!

Descending, she led the way to a spring which gurgled merrily at the foot of the hill, feeding a little rivulet which wound its way bashfully among the trees, heading toward the larger stream which we had crossed before entering the woods. Here we sat down under a great tree, which had been felled by the relentless axe of some woodman in bygone years. Its branches had fallen off and decayed, but the mighty trunk remained almost intact, affording a pleasant rustic seat. For a long time we talked, discussing thoroughly all the matters of interest between us. In turn we gave attention to mission work among the poor, the liquor traffic, gambling, the publication of scurrilous literature and other social reform questions. And then we discussed the money question, the tariff, monopolies and other matters of interest to our government. In most particulars we agreed, but in some we did not. It must have been a queer sight to the robins that were mating above our heads. We gesticulated as earnestly and spoke as excitedly at times, as though the salvation of the republic depended upon our efforts right then and there.

"Miss Thorne, pardon my abruptness," said I at length; "but I wish to say frankly that I am charmed with you. I have read quite extensively, conversed with many able men, and traveled from one ocean to the other, but I have never found one so uniformly well-posted on all subjects, nor so sensible in conclusions as yourself. Your versatility amazes me, and I wish to know the secret of your achievement."

"A sound mind in a sound body, Doctor, and then hard work," said she. "It is no secret. And yet, I am sure you over-estimate me. I am only a simple girl, seeking light, and trying to be useful."

Then, thought I, heaven give us more simple girls! It was dawning upon me just then that this lady in bloomers was more to me than any other woman had ever been. I did not realize it, but felt myself irresistibly led into something far more than friendship for her. As her pretty, warm hand lay idly on the folds of that much-despised garment, the defense of which has cost many good men and pure women the ridicule of fashion's elect, I felt an almost unconquerable desire to take it in my own. But I hesitated, and changing the subject adroitly, she said:

"Where do you purpose spending your vacation this year, Doctor?"

"It is at present my intention to spend a week at Niagara, another at Toronto, and then a month among the Thousand Islands and along the St. Lawrence as far down as Quebec, perhaps. But it is some time yet before I secure leave of absence, and I might change my plans."

"I suppose your work is very heavy. I believe you wrote me that your congregation numbered 1,000 members. To care for so large a church must certainly consume a vast amount of nerve force."

"I need a helper, Miss Thorne," said I.

And I was about to say that I knew of no one in the skies above or on earth beneath that would fill all requirements as well as she. But I hesitated. Just that moment a sturdy old farmer appeared on the scene and my opportunity was gone. He was hunt-

ing a lost cow, he explained, and, describing her,
asked if we had seen anything of such an animal.
We had not, and so he went on, merrily whistling
"Auld Lang Syne" or some such tune, I've forgotten
just what.

"It is high time we were returning," said Miss
Thorne, consulting her little gold watch that nestled
beneath her belt. "Mamma will have dinner just at
seven, and it is now six."

We walked leisurely homeward, still talking reforms. But secretly I longed to change the subject
and discuss something more soothing to the affections. My heart yearned to whisper its love to those
pretty pink ears. Wait till you come to the little
rustic bridge again, said a voice within. Then for a
few minutes my pulse beat more normally; but when
we came in sight of the spot set for the conquest, my
foolish heart fairly pounded, and my face flushed
with excitement. I felt that the supreme moment of
my life had arrived. To win this fair girl's affections meant home, peace, sunshine, bliss!

As we stepped upon the bridge it seemed to sink
beneath our feet, for at the farther end there stood
three young street gamins angling for the little sunfish we had seen when passing over. Once again my
plans were foiled. My heart ached.

"Good evening, boys," said my friend pleasantly.

"Good evening, Miss Thorne," said the urchins in
concert.

"How do they bite?" said she.

SITTING UPON THE LOW DIVAN SHE PLAYED.—
Page 118.

"Oh, tip top!" said the eldest. "I've caught six already, and Billy and Jack have pulled in nine between 'em."

And, snipping the wings and legs from another grasshopper, he quickly re-baited his hook, and swishing the line a time or two about his head, the young fisherman let it fall far out in the stream, remarking with a wink that he was "figurin' on a black bass for a change."

"Three of my Sunday-school boys," explained Miss Thorne as we walked on. "I have a very interesting class of twenty just such fellows. They are all poor and uncultured, but some of them are very bright and promising. Rain or shine, hot or cold, they seldom miss a service. I've taught the class three years now, and visited often in the homes of the boys, most of whom I picked up on the street and induced to attend by promises of sweetmeats, picnics, or money. They have been very faithful to me, and seem to think everything of their teacher, and I'm sure I do of them. I'll tell you more about it some time, for I know you would be 'nterested in the story. But here we are at the stile again."

It lacked fifteen minutes of the dinner hour. Noticing a guitar leaning against the piano, I asked who played it.

"Sister and I both, a little," was the reply.

"Good! Then will you not favor me with a selection or two?"

Sitting upon the low divan, she played, at first a few of the old tunes familiar to all performers on this delightful instrument, and then something more modern. She had worn a waist of some white, soft material during the afternoon, with short open sleeves and low neck. As she swept the strings of the instrument with the abandon of a master, her soul in perfect accord with the sweet notes which she spoke into life and power, I thought I had never seen such a picture. And when she sang, at first a lullaby, and then some dreamy Italian love piece, I could hardly resist the impulse to go and sit down by her side, and, folding her to my bosom, declare all that I felt. But I hesitated. And it was well that I did, for within two minutes her good father appeared, and heartily greeting me, led the way to the dining room.

"By the way, daughter," said he to Miss Grace, as we sat at the table, "I have a letter for you."

"Oh, it's from Mrs. Brown," said she, hastily scanning the envelope. "Pardon me if I open it, as it may contain something of interest to us all."

It was a short letter and quickly read. Mrs. Brown had arranged for a meeting of the Chicago Social Science Club, of which she was president, at her residence the following week, Thursday afternoon. She desired that Miss Grace should be present and read a paper. Could she not come and spend a week or two?

My heart leaped with joy. She would accept the invitation, and I would see her often during the visit, for at no home in the city was I more welcome. My acquaintance with this winsome lass of the northland had become an affair of the heart with me, and there was no denying it.

"Shall I go, papa? What do you say, mamma? Will you take my Sunday-school class, sister?"

One question followed another, and all were satisfactorily adjusted. Yes, she would go, and as I would arrive home Saturday, would I please bear a message to Mrs. Brown and assure her of the pleasure with which her invitation was accepted.

The evening passed all too quickly. At eleven Jim arrived with the carriage, and I took my leave. Promising Miss Grace that I would meet her upon her arrival in the city, I gently pressed her hand, feeling that life was very sweet, but that it would never be quite perfect till this girl in bloomers, who daily was becoming more and more to me—a study of perpetual delight—should hear my declaration of love, and permit the caresses I longed to give.

A MEMORABLE GATHERING.

CHAPTER V.

A MEMORABLE GATHERING.

"There has fallen a splendid tear
  From the passion flower at the gate.
She is coming, my dove, my dear;
  She is coming, my life, my fate;
The red rose cries, 'She is near, she is near';
  And the white rose weeps, 'She is late';
The larkspur listens, 'I hear, I hear';
  And the lily whispers, 'I wait.'"
                                —TENNYSON.

My good people said that I preached with unusual power the following Sunday. Whether it was the run to the country, or a sudden inspiration, they could not say, but both my morning and evening sermons were fine, they declared. I was encouraged by the kind compliments, but surmised that it was not the country, nor any unusual inspiration in the orthodox sense that enabled me to do better pulpit work than usual, if I had done so, but the quickening power of a new-born love. And I was happy.

Although but three days till Miss Thorne was due, it seemed an age as I sat by my study window Monday morning. I could not work. My books looked uninviting and the room seemed close. I accordingly took my hat and cane and sauntered forth. I visited the park awhile, and then lunched down town. During the afternoon I paid many visits among the poor. I had never enjoyed the task so much as on this occasion. Was it the thought of three urchins catching sunfish and their sweet-faced teacher in a far off northern town that spurred me on? Perhaps.

At last the days dragged by, and I found myself in waiting at the station. The train was an hour late, and I writhed. Where was the patience of Job, which I had so often recommended in my sermons? Ah, well, I mused; Job never waited for a late railway train, nor loved a girl in bloomers. Besides, it is harder to practice a virtue than it is to preach it.

When the long train pulled in, I had no difficulty in finding my friend among the hundreds of passengers, for she was the only lady in bloomers. Clad in a light grey suit, with leggings and hat to match, she was the observed of all observers as she accepted my arm and walked with me down the long platform and ascended the stairway to the cab. She impressed me as a bird on wing, a ship under full sail on a friendly sea—poetry in motion! But others evidently were not impressed so favorably, for in passing the ladies' waiting room I heard an old witch say:

"Look there, Mirandy! Did you ever see the likes in your life? If that gal was my darter, I'd tan her hide and make her live on bread and water for a week. Such clothes!"

You would have your bony old hands full, old woman, thought I, as I glanced at the splendid creature beside me, and felt the great, warm muscular arm as the crowd pressed us together. Miss Thorne either did not hear the remark of the old way-back, or else cared nothing for it, as she kept up a merry chat, interrupted here and there with a ripple of laughter. She was evidently used to being talked about, and like the brave, true woman that she was, paid no more attention to it than to the blowing of the wind.

"Are you tired?" I asked.

"Oh, no!" she said. "I never get tired. Why should one? There is a sensible limit line to all endurance, and a wise person will never cross that line. Many do, I know; and in this way the maledictions of good people are induced against bicycling, bathing, football and other exercises. But how about that wheel, Doctor? Have you invested yet?"

"I should think you could surmise from the unusual stiffness of my gait," said I. "And if you only knew of the bruises! Yes, I purchased a high-grade safety day before yesterday, and have taken two lessons. I rode three blocks without falling this morning, and think it will not be long until I can get around very nicely."

"Bravo!" said she. "The next time you visit the villa we will be able to take a spin."

"I hope so."

We spent the evening with the Browns. The banker and myself facetiously begged the privilege of being present at the meeting of the club the following day, but were denied.

"Strictly for ladies," said Mrs. Brown.

"But we want to hear Miss Thorne's paper," said I.

"I shall take pleasure in rereading it to you and Mr. Brown some evening before my return if desired," said the obliging young lady.

"It is most urgently desired," said the banker.

It was a brilliant gathering that graced the spacious and elegantly furnished parlors of the Brown mansion the following afternoon. Fully a hundred of Chicago's fairest and brainiest women, married and single, came from the North, South, and West sides, arrayed in costliest silks and satins and bedecked with jewels. The street was lined with elegant carriages, and the whole affair appeared to be one of extraordinary splendor. All this I could guess as I looked out of my study window, which was in full view of the Browns, only a block away, and on the opposite side of the boulevard. Papers were read on various phases of dress reform, the subject that had been selected for the present meeting of the club. All were commonplace, however, simply following the old lines of a discussion that

FULLY A HUNDRED OF CHICAGO'S FAIREST AND
BRAINIEST OF WOMEN.—Page 126.

has been worn threadbare because of the impracti-
cabilities advocated, until Miss Thorne's name was
announced. And as one of the great dailies had sent a
special lady reporter to write-up the meeting, I cannot do better perhaps than to quote that portion of
the article which has to deal with my study. It appeared the following morning, copiously illustrated
from instantaneous photographs taken on the spot,
and caused a sensation:

"For many years American women have talked
dress reform, but few have practiced anything sensible on the subject. Consequently very little has
been accomplished. But there is one young woman
in our great land whose brave, true words and beautiful example have set the gossips talking with the
probability of good results. This young woman was
present, and was happily introduced by Madam President as 'Miss Grace Thorne, of Smithville, Wis., a
personal friend, whom I am sure deserves to be
ranked as one of the fairest living exponents of the
new womanhood.'

"And she does. Modest, brainy, well-sexed, beautiful,—certainly she made a fine appearance as she
stepped before that august gathering of Chicago's
best women. There was a general flutter for a few
moments when it was discovered that the speaker
was clad in bloomers. They were made of plush-
purple, more closely cut than last year's style, snugly
gathered below the knee, and almost hidden from

view by a very short skirt of the same material. The hose were of black silk, and displayed a limb as plump and perfect as sculptor ever carved. The waist was made of silk, with full sleeves, low neck, and bright trimmings. She wore no corset, yet presented a dream of loveliness in form seldom if ever surpassed. In introducing she quoted the words of Milton:

'Accuse not Nature: she hath done her part.
Do thou but thine.'

In a rich, well-modulated voice, she read, and her entire audience seemed hypnotized, so eagerly did they drink every word, and so enthusiastically did they applaud.

"'All women desire to be beautiful,' she said. 'Few are. All desire to be healthy. Few are. Why? Because the laws of nature are set aside, and senseless rules substituted. The ill-health of females is something appalling to-day. What are the causes? Among them have been enumerated—

Improper ventilation.
Unhygienic food.
Dearth of fresh air and sunshine.
Lack of exercise.
Over-work, over-study, and mental strain.
An abnormal nervous development.
Improprieties of dress.

A volume might be written under each of these

heads; but I must confine myself to the last on this occasion, and, by request of your worthy president, particularly to the corset. An irrational dress is the undoubted cause of much of the organic disease among our sex. A distinguished specialist says that '90 per cent of the so-called female diseases have their origin in corsets and heavy skirts. They not only depress the pelvic organs by their pressure and weight, but weaken all their normal effects.' It has been falsely said that 'every woman by mere structure is a life-long invalid.' That is a travesty on womanhood and truth. It is as natural under normal conditions for a woman to be well and strong as for man. Woman's 'weaknesses' should be denominated woman's follies.

"'Dr. Dio Lewis, in classifying the errors of woman's dress, speaks as follows:

"'First. The corset, which reduces the waist from three to fifteen inches and pushes the organs within downward.

"'Second. Unequal distribution. While her chest and hips are often overloaded, her arms and legs are so thinly clad that their imperfect circulation compels the congestion of the trunk and head.

"'Third. Long, heavy skirts, which drag upon the body, and impede the movement of the legs.

"'Fourth. Tight shoes, which arrest circulation, and make walking difficult. High heels, which increase the difficulties in walking, and so change the center of gravity of the body as to produce dislocations in the pelvic viscera.'

" 'This eminent authority is wise when he puts the corset at the head of woman killers, and makes it the twin-sister of the long skirt. The statistics of London corset dealers show that the average size of the female waist has decreased by two inches during the last quarter century. Dr. Ellis says: "The practice of tight lacing has done more within the last century toward the physical deterioration of civilized man than has war, pestilence, and famine combined." Another physician writes: "Woman, by her injurious style of dress, is doing as much to destroy the race as is man by alcoholism." Dr. Kitchen declares that "this appliance kills slowly, and, to the unlearned, imperceptibly; nevertheless the corset on a child is slow murder of the child. Every woman who has grown up in a corset, no matter how loosely worn, is deformed." Miss Frances E. Willard says: "But woman's everlasting befrilled, bedizened, and bedraggled style of dress is to-day doing more harm to children unborn, born and dying, than all other causes that compel public attention. With ligatured lungs and liver as our past inheritance and present slavery, the wonder is that such small heads can carry all we know! Niggardly waists and niggardly brains go together. The emancipation of the one will always keep pace with the other; a ligature around the vital organs at the smallest diameter of the womauly figure means an impoverished blood supply in the brain, and may explain why women scream when they see a mouse, and why they are so terribly afraid of a term which should be their glory, as it is that of their brothers, viz., strong-minded."

" 'The small boy in a school composition spoke truthfully, if not learnedly, when he said : "Girls kill the breath with corsets that squeeze the diagram. Girls can't run or holler like boys because their diagram is squeezed too much. If I was a girl I'd rather be a boy, so I could run and holler and have a good diagram." It has been argued that it is not natural for woman to breathe abdominally like man, and therefore the corset is no impediment to her development in this respect. But Dr. Kellogg has shown conclusively the fallacy of this theory by a series of careful investigations. He declares that "women who have never worn tight clothing breathe abdominally, as do men, and that civilized women who have formerly worn corsets, after having modified their dress in accordance with the demands of health, subsequently acquire the abdominal type of respiration."

" 'Personally, if I may be allowed to speak of myself, I do not know the effects of corset-wearing, as I have never had one on. For years, however, I have worn a light, snug-fitting waist, devoid of whalebone, metal, or other hard material. It is similar in appearance and make-up to the average corset-waist, yet more substantially and artistically made. My dressmaker fits it to the form, but is always cautioned not to make it tight at any point. The result is that I breathe abdominally, am free from any of the usual diseases attendant upon tight lacing, and am as strong as any average man of the same weight. When we allow the form to develop itself naturally, there will be no need of padding, which has become one of the worst fads of recent years in woman's make-up. It is the thwarting of the plans of nature by a slavish devotion to the ruinous rules of Dame Fashion that weakens woman physically and mentally in these days, and makes her the constant victim of designing quacks. Every woman ought to be strong. It is her right, and whatever fashion keeps her down should be stamped out in righteous indignation. One of woman's great missions is to be graceful, in all that this much-abused word implies. Goethe well says that "the highest grace is the outcome of consummate strength." It is wrong to blame the men for any irrational style of dress among women. The average well-sexed man detests a wasp-like waist. And was there ever one who did not abhor long trains, that modern pest of weddings and receptions? Oh, sisters, let us have done with all this nonsense. Discard corsets, long skirts, tight garters, cramping shoes, and every other thing that in any way impedes the fullest and freest development of the body. Every corset and long skirt ought

WHEN WE ALLOW THE FORM TO DEVELOP ITSELF
NATURALLY, THERE WILL BE NO NEED OF PAD-
DING.—Page 134.

to be relegated to the rag picker or the curiosity shop before the dawn of the twentieth century. It would mean more than pen can tell for our personal pleasure in living, for our homes, for our purses, for our posterity, and for all that is good, and beautiful and true.'

"At the conclusion of the paper all parliamentary rules were ignored for a time, and with one accord the ladies present moved forward to congratulate this splendid exponent of the better womanhood now dawning over a long-suffering world. The enthusiasm amounted to an ovation, and Miss Thorne may pride herself in stirring up the elite ladies of Chicago as they have never been stirred before. We shall no doubt hear of anti-corset clubs now in various parts of the city, and it will not be surprising to see many of our leading ladies arrayed in bloomers at no distant day."

Having an engagement in a distant part of the city that evening, I did not get to call at the Brown mansion until the next afternoon. Then Miss Thorne was out, and, worst of all for me, had accepted an invitation to spend the evening with one of the first families of the South side. Mrs. Brown recounted to me all the details of our mutual friend's triumph, and kindly invited me to dine with them the following day. It seemed to me the next twenty-four hours never would drag by. I walked the floor, looked out of my window, wrote a few letters, tried to read, and

did a variety of things, but found it impossible to
sleep until long after midnight.   Then I awoke early,
breakfasted, and, donning a sweater, gave myself up
to that new bicycle which I earnestly desired to master for her sake, if for nothing else.

Promptly at six o'clock I reached the Brown residence.   I went early, hoping to have a quiet hour
with Miss Thorne before dinner.   I was not disappointed.   After the usual preliminaries, our good
hostess left us alone, and we were permitted to con-
verse uninterrupted until the arrival of the banker,
fifty minutes later.

"Permit me now to congratulate you, Miss Thorne,"
I said, extending my hand, "over your splendid success Thursday.   I read the reports of the meeting in
the city papers with great interest, and especially
the synopsis of your paper."

"Thank you," said she, modestly accepting my
hand.

What a hand!   Just for a moment I held it, and
then reluctantly gave it up.   So perfectly shaped!
So pink with rich blood!   So firm!   So warm!

"Like the majority of people, I have taken but little interest in the subjects discussed at your meeting until I met you at the Villa," said I.   "Since then
I have read everything I could find bearing on the
matter, and am more and more persuaded that you
are fighting on the right side in a good cause.   At
first your ideas shocked me.   Bloomers I thought

were horrible. Riding a-straddle was almost unmentionable. The taking of vigorous exercise, the same as the sterner sex, had never entered my mind as being practicable or desirable for women. And as to corsets, I had heard my mother and sisters defend them on one or two occasions, and supposed of course that they were quite proper. But I am ready to confess that I am now a complete convert to your new womanhood ideas, and only wonder why everybody else is not.'"

"It is a very difficult thing to change long established customs," said she. "No matter how senseless and even sinful a thing may be, if it has been long accepted by the million, people cling to it with religious tenacity. And then, again, capital often opposes progress. As in the days of Paul the idol-mongers of Ephesus opposed his preaching because it hurt their business, so now the manufacturers scoff at those who advocate dress reform, and, as usual, the people are duped. But when once the eyes of Americans are opened to the prevalence of any great evil, and the conscience fully quickened, it is but a question of time when reformation follows, quick, sure and steadfast. I see just before us a better day for the women of our country. Certainly they will not much longer content themselves with being the slaves of the numerous customs which are now dragging thousands to untimely graves."

But I did not care to continue this discussion further just then. I had something else in mind; but just how to present it I did not know. I thought of my lonely evening the day before, and said:

"I was over to see you yesterday evening, and was sorely disappointed at finding you out. But I trust you had a delightful time."

"I was royally entertained," she said; "but cannot say that the experience was delightful. I am not much given to society as she is. There were long trains, decolette dresses, silly conversations, and insipid smilings and bowings. Everything was stilted. The women were laced within an inch of their lives, and the men were soaked in champagne. They all danced till a very late hour, and when they said their simpering good-byes they looked like wilted flowers from which the beauty and fragrance had flown forever. When I refused to dance, they had no better manners than to stare at me in amazement. I was really glad when the affair was over, and Mr. Brown led me to the carriage."

"How did you amuse yourself during the evening if you did not dance?" I inquired.

"The hostess kindly showed me through the library, art gallery and conservatory, which occupied some of the time; and then I met a number of interesting personages with whom I conversed. By the way, do you know a Mr. Sidney Vincent?"

"The railroad man?" I asked. "Yes, he is first vice-president of one of the great trunk lines leading out

THEY ALL DANCED TILL A VERY LATE HOUR.—
Page 140.

of Chicago. Was he there? He is a very talented and very wealthy gentleman."

"So I surmised," said she. "And he is quite young for one so distinguished. He is very versatile, and I really enjoyed my conversation with him, which can-not be said of any the others I met. He accompanied the hostess and myself in our rounds of the house, and I was surprised at the knowledge of books, paint-ings and flowers he displayed."

"Yes, he is a man of many parts," I remarked. "He was a member of my church before the disaffection caused by my tirade against sins in high life last fall, and we were good friends. But since then we seldom meet, as he withdrew from my congregation at the time."

"He seemed to be on warm terms with Mr. Brown," she continued, "and in response to the banker's invi-tation promised to dine with us some evening next week."

"Ahem!" was all I could say, immediately changing the subject by referring to an article of special inter-est in one of the late magazines. I had come over with the intention of declaring my love, but the Vin-cent episode had driven the resolution far from me. Perhaps it was just as well, for Mrs. Brown came in shortly after, and if I had attempted the declaration, she would undoubtedly have caught me in the very act.

The days flew past. I saw my study often, and

with ever-increasing admiration. But others saw her too, much to my unrest. Two or three admirers from other cities called to see her, and a half dozen or more from Chicago. But among them all none were so attentive as Mr. Sidney Vincent, the railroad magnate. He took her out to swell receptions, to the theater, and to hear great lecturers. She came with the Browns to hear me on Sundays, and always seemed glad to see me when I called, as I did quite regularly. I had become a fairly good rider by this time, and on several occasions we went cycling together. Her visit was prolonged two months or more, and still I seemed no nearer that declaration I so longed to make than I had been at the beginning. She was under no obligations to me, and yet I was intensely angry that she should receive the attentions of Vincent so continuously. But I managed to hold my tongue, nurse my jealousy, and so avoid a rupture.

"Well, Doctor, I'm going home to-morrow," she said one evening as I was making my accustomed call at the Browns.

"You don't say!" said I. "I'm very sorry."

"Why should you be?" she asked.

"Because I've taken great pleasure in your company, and have been profited exceedingly by your conversation."

"Thank you, Doctor; and permit me to say sincerely that your feelings are fully reciprocated."

Here was a good place to say what I had so long concealed. But I hesitated, and five minutes later the butler announced that Mr. Sidney Vincent was at the door, and would Miss Thorne be pleased to take a drive with him?

She did not seem anxious to go, I thought. But as she could not well refuse, she excused herself from me, and hastened to her room to prepare for the drive.

"One moment," said I, as she was leaving the parlor. "If agreeable, I will accompany you to the station to-morrow?"

"Oh, thank you! I should be delighted to have you do so, had other arrangements not been made. I neglected to tell you that Mr. and Mrs. Brown had suddenly decided to run out to the Villa to-morrow also, and Mr. Vincent has kindly offered to take us all together in his private car."

"Then, good-bye," said I, extending my hand. "I shall be very busy to-morrow, and will probably not see you again. Express my kindest regards to your parents and sister, and may you have a merry journey home."

She took my hand, and I imagined that her clasp was more prolonged and firm than was actually necessary according to established custom. And there seemed to be a look half akin to sadness in those deep, blue eyes, as she said:

"Good-bye, Doctor. I shall never forget your many kindnesses, and encouraging words. I hope you will visit us again at Smithville, and that at no distant day."

She was gone, and with heavy heart I retired to the library, until she and Mr. Vincent drove out of sight. Then I wearily took my departure, only to spend a sleepless night in my lonely room.

DIVERGING PATHS.

CHAPTER VI.

DIVERGING PATHS.

"We met, hand to hand,
  We clasped hands close and fast,
As close as oak and ivy stand;
  But it is past;
Come day, come night, day comes at last."
—ROSSETTI.

During July the weather was simply suffocating. My work dragged, and my health declined rapidly. From some unaccountable reason I had not felt so poorly in years, and I evidently looked like a corpse, for my Official Board voted unanimously to allow me a three months' vacation. An assistant pastor was secured to begin work immediately, and so on the first day of August I packed my trunk and left the city.

First I visited the old home in Kentucky.

"Poor Frank," said my gentle mother, as we sat in the family room the first evening after my arrival. "You have been working too hard."

I made no reply, but secretly upbraided myself for not telling her all about my sweet girl in bloomers. It did not seem wise to divulge particulars, however, so I kept my own counsel.

"Lor' bress my soul, chile, what's de matter?" said old Aunt Dinah, as with arms akimbo and wide-open eyes she stared at my pale, hollow cheeks and lank form. "You'se done and preached yerse'f to death, honey. Time you'se comin' back to old Kaintuck to git some flesh on dem bones. Dat city grub am no good. Takes Aunt Dinah's hoe-cake to chirk you up."

Evidently I had changed considerably in appearance, for few of the old neighbors knew me. The first morning after my return I took a stroll down the lane, and called at the humble home of a versatile old colored friend, known far and near as Deacon Ham. The good old man, a relic of slavery times, was sitting on a low stool in the luxurious shade of a gigantic elm. He was smoking some leaf-tobacco of his own raising and drying, and seemed at peace with all the world.

"Good morning, Deacon," said I, slapping the old fellow familiarly on the shoulder.

"Howdy, sah," said he, scrutinizing my face with a look of uncertainty.

"Why, Deacon, don't you know me?" I asked.

"Your voice sounds similar, chile," said he, still studying my features; "but I can't jist organize ye."

For the first time in a month I laughed heartily. Then I made myself known, and the old man was so chagrined to think of his failure in recalling my face and name that he fairly outdid himself in hospitality, hoping thereby to make amends. He cut the biggest

A RELIC OF SLAVERY TIMES WAS SITTING ON A
LOW STOOL IN THE LUXURIOUS SHADE OF A
GIGANTIC OAK.—Page 150.

watermelon he could find in the patch, and entertained me with a prodigality as amusing as it was surprising.

For ten days I tarried under the paternal roof, revelling in the scenes of my childhood. John Howard Payne spoke the sentiment of the whole wide world when he said,

"There is no place like home."

Now in the garden helping Aunt Dinah pick berries, eating two while I put one in the basket; then in the parlor, singing some sweet old duet with sister, while mother looked on with face all shining—heaven-kissed with light and love; again romping through the pastures gathering the pretty wild flowers, or sitting by the brook angling for perch, as in the good old times when I played truant from school, the days passed all too quickly. But I was restless, and decided to go on at once.

"Oh, please stay," begged sister. "It is so good to have you here,—good for us and good for you, brother. You know Longfellow says:

'Stay, stay at home, my heart and rest;
Home-keeping hearts are happiest,
For those that wander they know not where
Are full of trouble and full of care;
    To stay at home is best.'

Do stay until you are strong again, for it makes us all sad to see you looking so badly."

"I'll soon be all right, sister," said I, gaily. "A trip to the sea will do me good. You know I am very fond of salt-water bathing. And then the constant change of travel is exhilarating to me. No, I feel that I should go."

And so I went. First by rail to Toledo, where I took ship for Cleveland by way of Put-In-Bay. I shall never forget that ride across Lake Erie. It was a perfect day. The steamer was a palatial one, the waters placid, and the company jovial. During the afternoon light, fleecy clouds winged their way continuously beneath the deep blue background of sky which reached in unbroken wealth of color from horizon to horizon. An hour before we reached our destination the sun set. Its good-night rays stretched across the lake like great rods of gold, shimmering and glimmering on the spray in indescribable beauty. Sitting upon the upper deck, I drank in the splendor of the scene for miles, till an air of contentment I had not known for weeks possessed my soul.

Tarrying a day in busy Cleveland, I visited, among other places of interest, Garfield monument. Removing my hat, I stood for a long time before the ashes of our martyred president, musing on the strange freaks of fate. Here was a man than whom a more scholarly, efficient, patriotic and Christian never occupied the highest chair within the gift of his countrymen, suddenly cut down while in the

glory of his power, and this at the hands of an irre-
sponsible shadow of humanity. How cruel! And
yet in his death he perhaps exerted greater influence
in favor of the flag for which he had fought, and the
Bible by which he had lived, than he could have done
in a century of average living. God doeth all things
well, thought I, as I turned away. And yet in my
present frame of mind, with visions of a blue-eyed
bloomer girl flitting far from me in the private car
of a dashing young railroad king, I could hardly swal-
low my own theological medicine.

"He is playing a bold game," said I, soliloquizing.
"Well, we shall see. Knowing her as I do, I cannot
believe it possible that he will be successful. And
yet, why should he not be?"

From Cleveland I went to Chautauqua—gay Chautauqua, resort of the learned, the good and the happy
from all over this fair land. An exquisite lake 18
miles long, 1,290 feet above sea level, clear and cool,
its shores dotted here and there with pretty villages
and rural homes, certainly an ideal place for the
establishment of a world-renowned summer as-
sembly. Here I met numerous friends from Chicago
and other cities, and tarried several days, keenly
relishing the brilliant lectures, superb music, and
congenial society with which visitors to this remarkable spot are always regaled.

And yet I was not happy. Until that fatal night
when my love met Sidney Vincent, I felt that she

was mine. Our paths seemed to lead naturally into each other's and a union of bliss seemed sure. But now I felt that our paths were diverging, and a throbbing sadness I could not throw off possessed my heart. It seldom entered my mind that I was in any way to blame for the condition of affairs. Nor was she. It was cold, cruel, selfish Sidney Vincent whom I censured. But one evening as I was thinking it all over, as I had done a thousand times before, I said to myself, Why should I blame him? He is young, rich, attractive, bold. Grace Thorne is magnificent. Why should he not seek her hand? I do not deserve so fair a woman, for I am comparatively poor—poor in this world's goods, poor in health, and poor in resolve. She has been very friendly toward me because it's her nature, and she pities me. But when it comes to loving, why of course Sidney Vincent has the advantage every time.

In all of which I did my study a great injustice, not to mention myself. Diverging paths are generally dangerous.

Oh, for some one with whom to counsel! thought I. Since our good-byes were said nearly six weeks before, I had not mentioned my dear one's name to a living soul. Mrs. Brown? Why, yes! Why not write to her? Certainly. I will! Strange it has not occurred to me before.

And snatching a pen and some paper, I hastily penned the following lines to the banker's wife:

NIAGARA FALLS.—Page 159.

Chautauqua, N. Y., Aug. 15, 1896.

My Dear Mrs. Brown:

Here I am trying to enjoy my vacation. But I must confess to you that I am not happy. You once said that you wished Miss Thorne and myself might become more to each other than friends. At that time I was indifferent. But now I am madly in love. I have never told her so, and judging from the success of Mr. Sidney Vincent in monopolizing her company, presume I will never have the privilege of declaring my affections. I have never spoken of these things to a living soul before, and may be presuming on good nature to annoy you with them; but I must have counsel. Please write me at Toronto. I will be there in a few days. Tell me all.

Your Obedient Servant,

FRANK CHARLTON.

The next day I ran on to Niagara Falls. Securing comfortable quarters at a quiet boarding house, I sallied forth on my wheel. Crossing to Goat Island, I rode leisurely along the beautiful drive-way till I came to the Three Sisters. Here I dismounted, and cautiously made my way to a huge rock well out in the current only a short distance above the Canadian Falls. I did not contemplate suicide, but just wished to revel in the novelty and grandeur of the situation. Its very excitement was restful. The unceasing roar of the waters, like a thousand thunders, charmed me, and acted as a palliative to my troubled soul. Mrs. Sigourney's "Niagara," which I had often declaimed when a boy at school, came to mind, and, as there was nobody near, I could not resist the pleasure of repeating the matchless lines in my deepest orotund:

> "Flow on forever, in thy glorious robe
> Of terror and of beauty. Yea, flow on,
> Unfathomed and resistless. God hath set
> His rainbow on thy forehead, and the cloud
> Mantled around thy feet. And He doth give
> Thy voice of thunder power to speak of Him
> Eternally—bidding the lip of man
> Keep silence, and upon thine altar pour
> Incense of awe-struck praise."

During the next two days I visited numerous points of interest in the locality, such as Lundy's Lane Battle-ground, Brock's Monument, Whirlpool Rapids, the Devil's Hole, and the Cave of the Winds. I took a trip on the Maid of the Mist, as also on the electric railway which gives one a panoramic view of this wonderland for miles. I visited the islands at night, and enjoyed unspeakably that peculiar softness and sweet influence which comes with the moonlight when shed over a lovely scene. I tried to record my impressions and write a little description of the place for future reference, but failed in the attempt. For more than three centuries the pens of poets and prose-writers have fallen short of the task, which can never be adequately accomplished. So fascinated was I with the place that I would have remained longer, but for my anxiety to receive Mrs. Brown's letter which I had ordered addressed to Toronto. I had visited Niagara on several occasions before, but never with such interest. Was it my love for Grace Thorne that gave zest to everything this time? Perhaps, for the knowing ones assure us that love is synonymous with beauty and grandeur. A hundred times during the visit I had wished that my dear one were present. To have walked with her among the vine-twined trees of Goat Island, hand in hand; to have sat with her on some rustic seat in some quiet nook, breathing the love I had never dared to speak; to have driven with her to the mountain's summit or the Indian Village, and returned by moonlight—but, alas! Mr. Sidney Vincent's ghost forbade.

Taking an evening boat at the village of Lewiston, I enjoyed a seven miles' ride down the river, and thence out into Lake Ontario. This three hours' ride across the lake to Toronto was one never to be forgotten. For many miles before we reached our destination I stood on deck and watched the signal lights, which could easily be distinguished from those of the city. Commerce! Commerce! thought I. What a wonderful thing it has become since the days of Fulton, whose bravery to dare something new induced the ridicule of his countrymen. And then my mind reverted to bloomers and dress reform. Perhaps I did not think connectedly; but as in the days of Caesar all roads led to Rome, so at this time all my thoughts centered in Grace Thorne.

The next morning I was at the post office early. I was almost afraid to inquire if there were any mail for me, somehow doubting the probability of such a thing. But I inquired, and out came a letter! Postmarked "Smithville" too. Dear, good Mrs. Brown!

Hurrying to my room, I tremulously opened the missive and read:

Spring Rock Villa, Wis., Aug. 18, 1896.
My Dear Doctor Charlton:

You cannot know how pleased I was to receive your note, but sorry to hear of your unhappiness. It is unnecessary for me to assure you, I trust, that I sympathize with you fully, and shall do anything in my power to help you.

In the first place, I want you to know that while Mr. Vincent is a good friend of my husband's and myself, I should regret exceedingly to see him win the hand of Miss Grace. He is very attentive, 'tis true; but I have numerous reasons for believing there is nothing between them yet save friendship. He is undoubtedly very much in earnest, and intends declaring himself at no very distant day. But I honestly doubt whether she will accept him.

Miss Grace has been at home all summer, and visits me often, running out to the Villa on her wheel.

AS THEY ROWED IN PERFECT RHYTHM, THE LONG OARS FAIRLY
BENT BENEATH THEIR POWERFUL MUSCLES.—Page 165.

She is certainly as charming as ever, and to my mind the best all-around woman of the present day. She and her sister won first prize in a sculling race at Madison last week. There was a regatta there, and we all went down. Quite a number of ladies entered the contest, but among them all none were so fair and strong as our heroine. She and Josephine had been practicing for a month or more, and were in splendid trim. As they rowed in perfect rhythm, the long oars fairly bent beneath their powerful muscles. The crowd assembled to witness the races went wild with applause.

Next week Mr. Vincent will call at Smithville with his private car, and take the Thornes with him for a little outing in the great west. His mother and father will accompany them, and several business friends. It will be a merry little party I suppose. They will spend the entire month of September on the trip. Returning, Miss Grace is under promise to deliver some lectures in a number of Eastern cities. She has not been idle amidst all her sports, but what with writing for the magazines, and preparing some addresses on the great questions in which we are all so deeply interested, she has been very busy since her return from Chicago.

By the way, Doctor, why do you not write her? She has mentioned the matter two or three times to me, and seems somewhat hurt to think you cared so little for her. We often speak of you and I have been led more than once to surmise from casual remarks she has made, that you have a very warm place in her heart. Press your suit, and the prize is yours.

Sincerely your friend,

MRS. BROWN.

To say that this letter did me good is putting it mildly. Like water to a thirsty man in mid-desert, so were Mrs. Brown's encouraging words to me. Of course there were some things in the communication that were not calculated to allay my misgivings, for instance that month's trip to the great west. But the fact that she wished me to write her, and that Mrs. Brown thought activity on my part in pressing affection's claims could not but result in victory, cheered me immensely. I wrote immediately, a nice long letter, but void of sentiment, and addressed it to Smithville, hoping to reach her before her departure with the Vincent combination. I did not request, but suggested a reply. I stopped in Toronto a week, drinking in the charms of that fairest Canadian city. Not expecting any mail, I seldom went to the post office. But the evening before I was to leave, I strolled around that way, and received a lovely letter from Miss Thorne. She had enjoyed my communication very much, she said, and hastened to answer. She wrote at length concerning her doings since we had parted in Chicago, spoke solici-

tously of my health, and urged me to devote myself
assiduously to exercise, quoting the words of Dry-
den:

"Better to hunt in fields for health unbought,
. Than fee the doctor for a nauseous draught.
The wise for cure on exercise depend;
God never made his work for man to mend."

She concluded by wishing me a pleasant vacation,
and assured me that a letter from me would be
gladly received at any time. And more, she begged
that I would not forget that the "latch-string was
always out" for me at her home, and she hoped I
would see fit to remember them with a visit before
my return to active work.

For the first time in many weeks I was happy. A
spirit of confidence seemed to be brooding over me,
and life once more grew wondrously sweet. Leaving Toronto on one of the splendid boats that makes
traveling a luxury between Montreal and the West
during the summer, I disembarked at Kingston the
following day, and after a visit to the fortifications
which are the chief attraction of that sleepy old
town, proceeded toward Alexandria Bay through
the Thousand Isles. Securing pleasant quarters at
this far-famed resort, I settled down for a month's
solid rest and recreation. I soon formed congenial
acquaintances, and gave myself up to fishing, picnic
parties, long rides on the wheel and bathing. I had

never taken much interest in rowing, but now I threw myself into the sport with the zeal of a college man who knows more of oars than of books. A number of us got our heads together and improvised a gymnasium, and what with dumb-bells, horizontal bars, and sand bags, together with bowling, rowing and cycling, I soon regained my old-time vigor with much to boot. We made a number of century runs on our wheels, and long before the month was up I had the muscles of a pugilist and the color of a farm-hand.

The second week after my arrival at the Bay, I concluded to answer Miss Grace's letter, which I had carried next my heart ever since I had left Toronto. It was Sunday, and in the quiet of my room, which overlooked the majestic river, I expressed myself as follows:

Alexandria Bay, N. Y., Sept. 9, 1896.

My Dear Miss Thorne:

Allow me to say that your kind letter, received just before I left Toronto, gave me great pleasure. I beg your pardon for not having written sooner, and assure you that it was not because of any indifference on my part. No, I would rather correspond with you than anybody else. But I felt that perhaps letters from my pen would be an intrusion, and so did not write.

What a delightful time you have had during the summer! And yet how busy you have been. It must be exhilarating to be always at one's best, equally ready for work or play. This seems to be the case with you, and if this is one of your new-woman ideas, I say god-speed.

It is with pleasure I assure you that my health is becoming exuberant. And as to exercise, I'm becoming a regular crank. Yesterday I rode 100 miles on my wheel, and then rowed an hour before retiring. To-morrow a party of us are going out camping. We will take our guns, blankets, cooking utensils, and fishing tackle, and rough it for a week at least.

Were you ever at the St. Lawrence? I believe you told me once that you had never been. Well, it's the grandest river in the world without a doubt, and one of the most delightful spots on earth in which to while away the hot weeks of summer. This morning I was reading "Geraldine." I presume you have read that exquisite poem; if not, please permit me to send you a copy. The author spent many weeks in this fascinating locality, and perhaps a quotation or two from his lines might be interesting:

"Fair St. Lawrence! What poet has sung of its grace
  As it sleeps in the sun, with its smile-dimpled face
  Beaming up to the sky that it mirrors? What brush
  Has e'er pictured the charm of the marvelous hush
  Of its silence, or caught the warm glow of its tints
  As the afternoon wanes, and the even-star glints
  In its beautiful depths? and what pen shall betray
  The sweet secrets that hide from man's vision away

In its solitudes wild? 'T is the river of dreams.
You may float in your boat on the bloom-bordered streams,
  Where its islands like emeralds matchless are set,
And forget that you live, and as quickly forget
That they die in that world you have left; for the calm
Of content is within you, the blessing of balm
Is upon you forever.   Mortality sleeps
While you dream, an immortal; some mistiness creeps
Like a veil of forgetfulness over your past,
And it is not.   Your day is eternal, to last
Without darkness, or change, or the shadow of dread.
  Blessed isles where to-day and to-morrow are wed
In such fulness of bliss! Blessed river that smiles
In such beauty and peace by the beautiful isles!"

No wonder Holland loved to spend his summers
here. It is an ideal spot for poets, a veritable para-
dise for verse-makers and lovers. Ere you hear
from me again I will have shot the rapids—a most
exciting experience they say—and have visited Montreal and Quebec. I trust you may favor me with a
letter at the latter place, from which I will write you
previous to my departure on a long hunting trip up
in the wilds of British Columbia.

I presume you are now in the far west, enjoying
your trip to the utmost. It is very kind of Mr. Vincent to afford you such an opportunity, and I'm sure
you will make the best of it. I shall not be surprised if I read of your making free-silver speeches
to the Californians, and championing the movement
which favors Government ownership of railroads.

SIDNEY VINCENT.—Page 173.

Well, rest assured of my sympathy. You have a right to be heard on every great question, for your views are sensible, your ability remarkable, and your spirit commendable.

Miss Thorne, I cannot say all I would like to say at this time; but ere my return to work I hope to accept your invitation, and spend a little time with you in your hospitable home. Then I shall be able to speak what I cannot write, I trust, and we shall know each other better. Farewell.

Your Devoted Friend,
FRANK CHARLTON.

I tore this letter up and re-wrote it twice before mailing; and then hesitated lest the closing paragraph should prove too presumptions. I feared that before she received it perhaps Sidney Vincent would have her promise to wed, and then what a fool I would seem to both.

Oh, foolish man! Could you have seen the love-light dancing in those deep blue eyes as she read that self-same paragraph, your soul would have been filled with delight, and a peace unspeakable would have possessed your anxious heart.

A WOMAN'S PLEA FOR NATIONAL RIGHTEOUSNESS.

CHAPTER VII.

A WOMAN'S PLEA FOR NATIONAL RIGHTEOUSNESS.

"There ought to be a system of manners in every nation, which a well-formed mind would be disposed to relish. To make us love our country, our country ought to be lovely."—BURKE.

"Then none was for a party;
  Then all were for the state;
Then the great man helped the poor,
  And the poor man loved the great.

The lands were fairly portioned;
  The spoils were fairly sold;
The Romans were like brothers
  In the brave days of old."   —MACAULAY.

Five weeks passed. At Quebec I received letters from Mrs. Brown and Miss Thorne, both of which I answered at length, and then left for a long hunt in the virgin fields of the far north. There were ten of us in the party, all professional men seeking health and pleasure. We found both in rich degree. Sailing up the picturesque Saguenay as far as navigable, we bade good-bye to civilization and plunged into the trackless wastes of wood-land and prairie, and were abundantly rewarded with good shooting and exhilarating adventure.

It was the middle of October before we reached Quebec on the return trip. We had seen no papers, nor received any mail for a month. It took some

time to catch the pace of events once more. I purchased a ticket for Portland, and was soon under the
American flag again. Blessed stars and stripes!
How my heart leapt as my eyes once again feasted
on the glorious ensign. It is well enough to spend a
few weeks under the "Union Jack," but for steady
living give me "Old Glory" every time.

At Portland I received a letter from Miss Thorne,
in which she gave me a detailed account of her gala
trip through the west. Mr. Vincent's name was not
mentioned, for which I was grateful. She had visited many points of interest, and by invitation addressed enthusiastic dress-reform meetings in several cities. Returning she had arranged a lecture
tour through the east under auspices of the Women's
Christian Temperance Union, speaking at Cincin-
nati, Pittsburg, Buffalo, Albany, and Boston, from
which point she was writing me. The following
evening she was to speak in New York; thence
Philadelphia, Baltimore and Washington, from
whence she would return home.

She made no allusion to her reception in the different cities, modestly leaving that for me to find out
if I wished to know. But as nearly every paper I
picked up had something in its columns about Miss
Thorne, I had no difficulty in learning that she was
rapidly gaining in fame and influence. While some
journals condemned her and her work, the majority
commended. One or two of the funny papers

printed ridiculous cartoons, and dubbed her the "ty-rant in bloomers." But nevertheless vast throngs came to see and hear her wherever she spoke, and people of every rank were moved to better living by her earnest appeals in behalf of a higher manhood and womanhood. Dress reform clubs sprang up like magic in various cities, and thousands were led to adopt her simple style of dress.

"Can I reach Washington to-morrow evening by eight o'clock?" said I to the hotel clerk an hour after receiving her letter.

"You can by leaving here at five this evening," was the reply.

The time was short, but I determined to go. To hear Grace Thorne in one of her now famous lec-tures, and to feast my eyes once again on her lovely face and matchless form, would be indeed a pleasure well worth the effort.

I arrived at the capital in good season, and, se-curing quarters at the Arlington, hastened to the box office to see about a seat. To my chagrin, every seat was sold, and standing room at a premium, and this at the largest opera house in the city. Fortunately I found a man at the hotel who had been summoned out of the city by telegram, and gladly sold his ticket to me. It lacked yet an hour till the lecture, so I put in the time dining. Consequently, I was in a most peaceful frame of mind when I reached the great auditorium, and was shown to my seat, which proved to be in excellent range of the platform.

The band played several popular airs while a hundred distinguished ladies were taking seats on the stage and arranging preliminaries. Promptly at 8:15 the speaker appeared in company with her friend and mine, Mrs. Brown. A storm of applause greeted the heroine of the hour, and after a happy introduction by the wife of a noted congressman, a leader in social circles, Miss Thorne began. I did not take a single note, but think I can reproduce a tolerably perfect synopsis of the address, so simple was it, and yet so wondrously earnest and impressive. She was dressed in bloomers, as usual. Although not quite so stout as when I had last seen her, she was still the living embodiment of glorious health. Her eyes flashed with intelligence and depth of feeling as in a voice as melodious as it was powerful, she said:

"We are on the eve of a national election. It should be a matter of tremendous moment to every citizen. Every American, male and female, should be a politician. Not a partisan, but a student of the science of government. Great dangers threaten the welfare of our republic. History repeats itself. Some of the same evils that have figured in the overthrow of other nations are now preying upon our body politic. It is folly to cry, Peace, peace! when there is no peace. We have little or nothing to fear from without. All the powers of earth united could not cope with America in a struggle at arms. Our Yankee ingenuity, proverbial patriotism and indom-

WHITE HOUSE.

itable courage would rally to the support of the star-spangled banner and successfully defend it against all opposition.

"But we have much to fear from within. Nearly all the nations of antiquity fell because of internal corruption, and not from outward assault. One by one the great monarchies of earth have left the world's stage, and for six thousand years the hopeful have sighed in vain for an enduring government. When our forefathers crossed the stormy deep and blocked the United States from the wilds of a new continent, it was fondly prophesied that here in Columbia, fair virgin of the occident, would be realized the dream of the centuries.

"Watchman, what of the night?

"A cursory review of existing conditions cannot but arouse a feeling of alarm in every loyal heart.

"First, in this land of plenty, where the fertile soil is capable of producing food enough to feed every mouth in the world and plenty to spare if needs be for the inhabitants of other planets, four million men are idle fully eight months out of every twelve. Millions of bushels of wheat are stored in the elevators of the land, while their children all but beg for bread.

"In the second place, while the rich are becoming richer, the poor are becoming poorer. With seventy per cent of the wealth of the nation in the hands of 5,000 millionaires, it is safe to say that we are slum-

bering on the verge of a revolution more terrible
than history has yet recorded.

"Again, our long-boasted liberties are being impugned. An aristocracy of wealth is dominating
everything. Money, whether accumulated by fair
means or foul, will seat almost any demagogue in the
halls of legislation, where laws are enacted to suit
the favored few. So great has become the power of
wealth that almost every other ambition has been
obscured, and the advice of Ben Jonson is almost
universally heeded:

> 'Get money; still get money, boys,
> No matter by what means.'

"We are now twenty years into our second century as an independent power. Shall we be able to
pass through without disruption? It depends. There
are several gigantic wrongs that must be corrected
if we succeed. I will call attention to a few of these
wrongs, perhaps not in the order of their magnitude,
but simply as they occur to me.

1.—THE FINANCE QUESTION.

"What the blood is to the body, money is to the
nation. To insure health, the blood must be pure,
and there must be plenty of it. So to insure the old-
time prosperity of this country again we must have
honest money, and more of it. Prior to 1873 we had
free coinage of silver. Then this metal was demone-

tized, and a blow struck, the effects of which we have been feeling the past three years. Silver must be restored and the two metals maintained at a reasonable parity before we will ever see the prosperity for which we are all longing. That man who favors a single gold standard for this country is an enemy to his flag. He may not realize it, but foreign capital does. To-day vast American properties are controlled by English capital, a thing which never would have occurred under bimetallism. What our mother country failed to do with shot and shell, she is slowly but surely accomplishing with her gold. It is high time every American were awake. It is a question of votes, and he who loves his country will never cast another ballot for any man or party pledged to the Bank of England's policy as against American liberty and prosperity.

"Many have said they favored bimetallism providing we could induce Germany, France and other nations to go in with us and make the policy international, but that it would be suicidal for us to attempt it alone. Oh, my countrymen! Where is the patriotism of Washington, Jefferson, and Webster? Have we no courage left? Is it so bad as that? Heaven forbid that this, the richest and most powerful government on earth, should lick the hands of foreign capitalists, and, like a whipped spaniel, bide the sweet wishes of an unworthy superior. Unable to restore silver alone! Such talk is traitorous, and the politician who whines it in his canvass for votes should promptly be boycotted at the polls.

"And then we must have more money per capita. Think of transacting the vast business of 65,000,000 people on a scanty $25 per head! No wonder times are close, money hard to get and everything depressed. Elect a bimetallist president and Congress, restore silver, then double the circulation per capita within five years, and America will see a season of prosperity such as the sun has never looked down upon since the world began.

2.—PROHIBITION.

' 'Ha! see where the wild, blazing grog-shop appears,
  As the red waves of wretchedness swell;
How it burns on the edge of tempestuous years—
  The horrible light-house of hell!'

"Important as is the money question to America, the liquor question is more so. It touches us at every angle of our national life, only to blight, wither and curse. And yet for many years the politicians have cried, Moral suasion, moral suasion! The liquor question is one that properly belongs to morals, and should not be lugged into politics! But to my mind it is the greatest political question of the age. When we consider that there are in round numbers 250,000 saloons in America, which annually scoop into their tills $1,500,000,000—more than enough to pay the en tire public debt of the nation—it is treason to our higher interests to keep the saloon question out of politics. The dominant parties of the country have quarreled over the tariff for many campaigns. Stump orators have shouted themselves hoarse over the tariff, tariff, tariff! And yet it is a small question comparatively. A matter of only $278,000,000 in 1894, or less than one-fifth the amount directly involved in the saloon question. It is to the interests of brewers and distillers to keep up this everlasting talk about the tariff, for it serves well as dust with which to blind the eyes of voters. No matter if there is but five per cent difference between the Mills and McKinley bills, let them saw away, tweedle-dee and tweedle-dum, so long as the sacred interests of the still house are not tampered with!

"Few realize the enormity of this evil. Ex-Governor St. John estimates the number of drunkards who annually fill untimely graves in this country at 150,000. Think of it! During the civil war both sides lost 500,000 men. It was a calamity never to be forgotten. Yet in the same length of time we are now burying more victims of the wine cup, and this in a time of peace, and in a Christian land! Aside from this are to be considered the tens of thousands of sad-faced wives and ragged children, the blear-eyed poverty and hideous ignorance, and all the awful crimes caused by intemperance. In one year 3,000 wives lost their lives by the cruelty of drunken husbands. Ex-Governor Dix was not far wrong when he said, 'Intemperance is the undoubted cause of four-fifths of all the crimes, pauperism and domestic misery in the state of New York.' Gladstone declares that 'Intemperance has injured the Anglo-Saxon race more than war, pestilence and famine.' And Leopold, Duke of Albany, once asserted that drink was the only enemy England had to fear. What is true of the mother country in this respect is true of her giant offspring. 'While drinking continues,' said Mr. Livesey, so long ago as 1831, 'poverty and vice will prevail; and until this is abandoned no regulations, no efforts, no authority under heaven can raise the condition of the working classes. It is worse than a plague or pestilence, and the man is no friend to his country who does not lift up his voice and proclaim his example against it.'

"We take great pride in our public schools, and well we may. The little red schoolhouse is the arbiter of our destiny, the assurance of our prosperity in a very practical sense. And whatever power, social, political or ecclesiastical, that would threaten our school system should be summarily shorn of its head. We have millions invested in our school properties. And yet if to-night some wanton fiend from an unknown world should sweep across the continent with a mighty torch in hand and fire every public school building in the land, the drink bill of the country for fifty-two weeks would restore all with abundant interest!

Protection or free trade, hard money or greenbacks, if the saloons of America were closed to-morrow, never again to open, there would not be a loaf of bread, a pound of meat, or a suit of clothes left in the shops of the land when Saturday night came. There is no such thing as overproduction. Such a statement is a travesty on truth, a lie invented by political tricksters. Outlaw the whisky business, and legitimate trades would immediately experience the greatest revival in their history.

"But who is to blame for this state of affairs?

"Least guilty, the poor drunkard, whose depraved appetite drives him on from bad to worse, against reason, revelation and everything that is good and true.

"Next guilty, the saloonkeeper, brewer and distiller, who are all in it for the money. I'd rather be a thief than a dealer in liquors. A thief steals your watch, but he cannot harm your character, nor rob you of your ability to earn another watch. But the liquor dealer beats you out of your money, besmirches your character, chokes the life out of ambition, and generally damns both soul and body. A highway robber is a gentleman as compared with a man who makes or sells intoxicating beverages. The average murderer is a saint as compared with the fiend who deals out death poison over the bar of a grog shop, and slowly but surely kills his hundreds of victims.

"Most guilty, the voter who casts his ballot for license! I care not how pious you may be, and your liberality may be proverbial, but so long as you pray, 'Thy will be done,' and vote with license parties and for license men, Satan will have the cinch on your deluded soul. Crusades may be all right in their places; but I have little confidence in them. Resolutions to Congress, as a rule, are not worth the paper on which they are written. The need of the hour is for men to vote as they pray. Whisky men care more for one adverse ballot than for a thousand prayers without the ballot. Pray right and vote right, and any evil can be controlled. The only consistent ground for a Christian nation to take is prohibition, absolute, imperative, perpetual! And it is a question of life or death. Nearly all the great nations of antiquity died drunk. Can we hope to escape their fate much longer under existing conditions? Right is right. Saint or sinner, Christian or infidel, the man who loves his country will henceforth vote for prohibition.

3.—EQUAL SUFFRAGE.

"'Consistency, thou art a jewel.' We whipped England because she sought to enforce taxation without representation. And yet for a century we have perpetuated the same gross wrong in debarring the gentler sex from the rights of citizenship! It is

SENATE CHAMBER.

certainly one of the marvels of this enlightened age and nation that so palpable an injustice should be tolerated so long.

"But men say that woman cannot reason; that she has no business ability; and that politics is not her sphere anyhow, and therefore she should not be permitted to vote and hold office. This is a slander on history, to say nothing of the present. When has the world seen greater rulers than Marie Stuart, Elizabeth and Mary, Queen of Scots? And has not Victoria presided acceptably for fifty-five years over the greatest monarchy in the world? Did not Deborah turn the captivity of Israel into freedom and victory when there was not a man among the tribes capable of leading the hosts? Woman's achievements in science, literature and the arts is sufficient argument in the affirmative on the question as to her ability to reason. But even if she be considered man's inferior in this respect, she is his superior in intuition. Her sympathies are nearly always on the side of the right. It was a woman who designed the stars and stripes. It was a woman who wrote 'Uncle Tom's Cabin,' a work that did more to free the slaves than all the speeches, resolutions and legal measures of a century. It was a woman who first dared to banish the wine cup from the White House. And as to business ability, nine men out of ten owe their success in life to the economy, foresight and courage of their wives.

"A few years ago Senator Ingalls insisted that woman ought not to have the ballot, because she couldn't fight! His domestic experience has been a happy one, free from broken broomsticks and disheveled hair, and he is therefore to be forgiven for so reckless an assertion. But in the good days coming, when women will be as strong as men, there will be no room for this objection. However, there will be no occasion for woman's shouldering a musket and marching out to war, when she has the ballot, for she will arbitrate. And that is better.

"Mr. Ingalls says that equal suffrage is coming, much as he deplores it. He fears that politics will not do woman any good. Perhaps not; but woman will do politics good! Whatever woman has touched in the march of the centuries she has purified. It has always been her mission to clean up cobwebs and scrub. Give her a chance in the halls of legislation and some ugly laws now in force will be removed forever from the statute books of civilization. In Delaware and South Carolina, for instance, the age of consent is ten. In Wyoming and Kansas, where women have limited rights at the polls, the age of consent is eighteen. What she has accomplished under cramped privileges in these states she will duplicate with abundant interest in every state when she has an equal chance.

"Equal suffrage is coming. It is in the air. The best men of all parties admit it. Abraham Lincoln said, 'I go for all sharing the privileges of the government who assist in bearing its burdens, by no means excluding women.' Charles Sumner declared that 'In the progress of civilization woman suffrage is sure to come.' Why not? For, as William H. Seward said, 'Justice is on the side of woman suffrage.' Some time before his death the beloved Whittier wrote, 'For over forty years I have not hesitated to declare my conviction that justice and fair dealing, and the democratic principles of our government, demand equal rights and privileges of citizenship, irrespective of sex. I have not been able to see any good reasons for denying the ballot to woman.' In this he accorded perfectly with the great Wendell Phillips, who said, 'I take it America never gave any better principle to the world than the safety of letting every human being have the power of protection in its own hands. I claim it for woman. The moment she has the ballot, I shall think the cause is won.'

"Give woman the ballot and the sacred interests of her home and family will impel her to vote right on all great moral questions. The party that gives woman this just privilege will do a service for humanity not excelled in the annals of time. If we hope to live as a nation through our second century the sooner we discard all discrimination of sex, in religion, business and politics, the better.

4.—THE RACE QUESTION

Is a simple one, though broad and important. It should not be confined to the negro. Nor yet the Chinaman. America is the natural asylum for the depressed and oppressed of every land. So long as men come here with good intentions, so long should they be welcome, irrespective of color, religion or social position. The black man has as good a right to America as the white; the same is true of the yellow man, the red man and the Asiatic. But whoever asks admission at our gates, East or West, and is unwilling to conform to our habits, learn our language and become naturalized and patriotic American citizens, should be unceremoniously dismissed. The springing up of immense foreign colonies in our midst, where our language is despised, our Bible scoffed at, our flag trailed in the dust, and our institutions generally demeaned, is a menace of mighty magnitude. No party should be so anxious for votes as to wink at these things. Strict immigration laws should be enacted and enforced to the letter. 'America for Americans' should be the watchword of all.

"Oh, let us have done with playing government! Vast interests are at stake. We are making history. The welfare of millions in other lands, as well as our own, aye, the welfare of billions yet unborn, should incite us to action, quick, noble, sure. Imploring every voter to do his duty at the polls next

Tuesday, I would conclude with the gifted Holland's grandest sonnet:

" 'God give us men! A time like this demands
    Strong minds, great hearts, true faith, and ready hands!
    Men whom the lust of office does not kill;
    Men whom the spoils of office cannot buy;
    Men who possess opinions and a will;
    Men who have honor—men who will not lie;
    Men who can stand before a demagogue
    And scorn his treacherous flatteries without winking.
    Tall men, sun-crowned, who live above the fog
    In public duty and private thinking!
    For while the rabble with their thumb-worn creeds,
    Their loud professions, and their little deeds,
    Mingle in selfish strife, lo! Freedom weeps,
    Wrong rules the land, and trailing justice sleeps!' "

As she retired an avalanche of roses was hurled upon the platform, and thunders of applause shook the great building. Frequently during the address the brave and beautiful speaker had been interrupted with rounds of applause. But now it was simply deafening, irresistible, long-continued. It is safe to say that no such a scene had ever been enacted in that auditorium. Men cheered themselves hoarse and women waved their handkerchiefs. It was like a mighty cloudburst of enthusiasm, in which I found myself as deeply immersed as the rest.

At last the band struck up "My Country, 'Tis of Thee," and with one impulse the vast audience arose and joined in that soul-stirring hymn. It was wholly spontaneous and irregular, but the effect was electrical and far-reaching. When the verses had been sung, the people retired, many weeping from depth of feeling and holy emotions.

. I crowded my way toward the stage, hoping to meet my loved one. When within a few feet of a side entrance I happened to glance toward one of the boxes, when whom should I behold but Sidney Vincent and Banker Brown. They were evidently waiting for somebody. My heart sunk within me, every happy resolution was subdued, and, without waiting to see any more, I turned and left the building.

AMONG THE ROCKIES.

RIVER IN ROCKY MOUNTAINS.

CHAPTER VIII.

AMONG THE ROCKIES.

"Mountains are the beginning and the end of all natural scenery."—RUSKIN.

"Round its breast the rolling clouds are spread;
Eternal sunshine settles on its head."
                                        —GOLDSMITH.

"See the mountains kiss high heaven,
And the waves clasp one another."
                                        —SHELLEY.

It was perhaps foolish in me to leave the opera house so abruptly. How did I know that they were engaged? I surmised so, but perhaps I was mistaken. I could not blame Vincent for following her about and seeing as much of her as possible. And yet I wished he were in Guinea, and I had a monopoly of the attentions of Miss Grace Thorne, my study in bloomers.

Much dejected and worn with the long ride of the previous night and day, I threw myself into bed immediately upon reaching my room. And as I was now in the best of health, brown as a berry and as strong as a mule, I slept at once and soundly. It was late when I arose the next morning. I dressed leisurely and went down to breakfast, philosophizing on fate and kindred subjects.

"Here's your morning paper,' sir! All about the big speech by the woman in bloomers. Paper?"

"Yes, I'll take one. Here, boy!"

And I read. Column after column (for it was a long and carefully prepared report) I digested with the avidity of a starving Arab. The waiter brought my order, and gently called my attention to it twice before I concluded. And then so keen was my interest that all relish for my food was gone. But I went through the motion, mechanically bolting a good supply of beefsteak and hot rolls. Then I walked into the office and inquired for a time-card. When I arose my first impulse had been to hunt up the Browns and Miss Thorne and spend the day with them in viewing the sights of the capital city. But the paper stated that they had all left shortly after the address in Mr. Sidney Vincent's private car for a short tour through the South. So I decided to see Mount Vernon, and perhaps ascend Washington Monument, and then return to my work.

At ten o'clock I caught a steamer and enjoyed an hour's ride on the beautiful Potomac. Landing at Mount Vernon, I visited the tomb of our nation's greatest hero,

"The first, the last, the best,
The Cincinnatus of the West."

As I stood within a few feet of the sarcophagus containing his bones I was moved as never before with mingled feelings of patriotism, gratitude and hope. Visiting the old home of the General, whom Napoleon declared to be the greatest warrior of his age, I went reverently from one room to another, reading all the inscriptions and examining all the relics with a minuteness and pleasure I had never experienced in a similar study. Mount Vernon is the Mecca of Americans, and thanks to the women of the land, the sacred property is in a good state of preservation.

So deeply impressed was I with a tribute from the pen of Dr. Andrew Reed of England, which was exposed in one of the rooms, that I copied it, and cannot forbear reproducing it here:

WASHINGTON,
The brave—the wise—the good;
WASHINGTON,
Supreme in war, in counsel, and in peace;
WASHINGTON,
Valiant, without ambition;
Discreet, without fear;
Confident, without presumption.
WASHINGTON,
In disaster, calm; in success, moderate;
In all himself.
WASHINGTON,
The hero; the patriot, the Christian;
The father of nations, the friend of mankind,
WHO,
When he had won all, renounced all, and sought
in the bosom of his family, and of nature,
retirement, and in the hope of religion,
immortality.

The following day I departed for Chicago. Many
dear friends, tried and true, met me at the depot,
and the following Sunday I preached to the largest
audiences in the history of my pastorate. Everything had gone well in my absence, my assistant
having proven the right man in the right place. Even
the old sexton was contented, and once more I entered into the details of my exacting profession with
a zest of which I had imagined myself incapable.

The second Sunday I was surprised, upon entering my pulpit, to see the Browns once again in their
accustomed pew, and with them Grace Thorne! At
the close of the service none were more cordial in
their greetings than these dear friends.

"Why, Doctor, how stout you are! And how well
you look!" exclaimed Miss Thorne.

"The very picture of health," echoed Mrs. Brown.

"Shooting must agree with you," said the banker.
"You must come over to dinner to-morrow and tell
us all about it."

I agreed, and faithfully kept my promise. I gave
a full account of my wanderings, and then after
dinner insisted upon a similar service on the part of
my study. The banker and his good wife begged to
be excused, stating that when inviting me to spend
the evening with them they had forgotten a promise
already made to attend an anniversary celebration
in a distant part of the city.

"But perhaps Miss Grace can entertain you just

as well as if we were present," said Mr. Brown, with a wink at his companion.

"I will do my best," replied Miss Thorne, innocently.

"And when she does her best at anything she always succeeds," said Mrs. Brown.

I fear the color rose to the very roots of my hair. Certainly this was a pleasure unexpected. Now if Sidney Vincent don't come poking his unwelcome head in, thought I, ungenerously.

He didn't come, and for three hours we had the house all to ourselves. Blessed hours!

Miss Thorne was, contrary to the usual rule, as good a conversationalist as she was public speaker. Drawing her rocker close to the easy chair I was occupying, she looked me pleasantly in the face and began:

"Now you wish me to tell you about the Rockies, do you? Grand old mountains! It was one of the most delightful trips of my life. Mr. Vincent has been very kind to me. His private car is a palace on wheels, provided with every luxury, and he has been generous enough to extend me several invitations, together with my relatives and friends, to accompany him on various jaunts through our beautiful country.

"We left for the West September first, and were absent just a month. We went out by the northern route, taking in the Red River country and the great

grazing districts of Montana. Diverging to the
south, we spent several days in the Yellowstone
National Park, that wonderland of creation. Then
continuing, we visited the thriving cities of Helena,
Spokane Falls, Seattle and Tacoma. A ride on glorious Puget Sound was a pleasure that will linger in
memory as long as I live. At Portland we stopped
two days. We took a steamer and ran up the Columbia as far as The Dalles. On the left as we ascended was the great state of Washington, which
contains more iron than Pennsylvania, more forests
than Maine, and greater agricultural resources than
Illinois. Mount Ranier, Mount Hood and other lofty
peaks showed their snowy heads, while on the right
Mount Shasta and the rugged gorges of the Cascade
range attracted the eye. I was deeply interested in
the fish wheels, which, revolving by the force of the
current, scooped up vast quantities of salmon, with
which the tables of the East are supplied—the finest fish in the world. Portland is perhaps the
wealthiest city of its population in America, but not
so pretty to my mind as some others. I spoke to the
ladies of the city one night on my hobby, dress reform. The papers were kind enough to compliment
the meeting and the address. However, Doctor, I
am not sure that this means much. For just as often
the dailies of the country are on the wrong side of a
question as the right, and their antagonism is frequently more of a compliment than their commenda-
tion.

"Leaving Portland, we passed up the beautiful Willamette Valley, dotted here and there with happy little towns, between which lay some of the prettiest farms in the world. Also the Rogue River and Sacramento valleys are dreams of rural loveliness. And for splendid feats of engineering, the road across the Siskiyou range presented some samples hard to excel.

"We spent four days at San Francisco, metropolis of the West. We usually think of this city as the jumping-off place, and yet so vast in area is the United States that if we count in Alaska, San Francisco is just half way across from New York!"

All of which I knew quite as well as she, but so charmed was I with her easy, running chat that I saw it in a new and better light than ever before. I had not spoken till now, when, feeling that I ought to say something, I meekly inquired:

"Did you visit Chinatown?"

"Indeed we did, a large party of us, under the direction of an experienced guide and two policemen. We spent several hours exploring the dives and dens of this horrible locality, the like of which is nowhere else to be seen, I suppose, under the folds of the American flag. To think of 45,000 people huddled together in the space of a few blocks, living like vermin! What with gambling, opium smoking and other evil habits contracted from so-called Christian nations, together with his natural propensities to vice, the poor Chinaman seems well nigh doomed both for this world and the world to come. And yet a strict en forcement of the excellent laws already existing would do much toward removing the unpleasant features of Chinese immigration.

"We visited the Presidio Military Reservation one morning and witnessed a grand, full dress parade. Here Uncle Sam's soldiers appear at their best, you know. It is one of the largest posts in the country, and the fort is one of the strongest in the world. The hills about the Golden Gate are literally lined with mighty guns, and I do not believe all the navies in the world combined could run the gauntlet of our splendid defenses at the entrance of San Francisco Bay, which is the pride of our Western coast, and undoubtedly the finest harbor in the world.

"The parade was beautiful and exciting. The perfect marching of the infantry, the methodical movement of the artillery, the rhythmic action of the cavalry and the stirring music of the regimental band electrified me, and for a moment I could not restrain my tears. But when I thought of the awful meaning of real war I said: Ah! what a mistake is all this. It seems a sin to spend millions in the support of an army and navy, when tens of thousands of our fellow-citizens are begging for honest work and bread. Of course, we have a small army as com pared with those of European nations. But what of it? War has become almost an impossibility, so de-

structive have become its munitions. How much better for a burdened humanity if the nations of the
earth would lay down their arms and arbitrate all
disagreements. What right have I to kill my brother
just because he refuses to agree with me? Might
never made right, but the world has been slow to
think so.

"Yes, we visited Golden Gate Park, Sutro's Gar-
dens and Bath House, and the new Cliff House,
where we watched the seals for an hour or more. It
was a charming sight to see the big fellows sunning
themselves on the huge rocks, while the waves of the
mighty ocean played about them.

"Leaving San Francisco we traveled south through
the far-famed San Joaquin Valley, and, reaching Los
Angeles, tarried a day or two before running on to
San Diego and the Mexican Line. The 'City of the
Angels' is well named. To my mind it is one of the
prettiest, as it is certainly one of the most prosperous, cities on the continent. I like Southern California. It is our Italy. Its blue skies, equable cli-
mate, luxurious fruits, beautiful flowers and progressive people combine in making it one of the most
highly favored spots in the Western hemisphere.
Southern California is the flower garden of the
world. To see calla lilies blooming out doors the
year round; to revel in the fragrance of orange blos-
soms perpetually, while enjoying the fruit; to dwell
in a pretty upland home where frost and fog are un-

known, and where the wild flowers wreathe the hills with a prodigality possible only to nature when in her happiest mood, are some of the privileges of this fairyland, which, however, is too far from the hub of civilization to suit one of my temperament if I were seeking a permanent home.   ,

"It is a great country for alfalfa, a sort of hay which grows six or eight crops a year if the ground is well irrigated. Speaking of this, reminds me of a story I heard on a tall, lank, lantern-jawed Missourian, who was visiting California for the first time, and had not yet become familiar with the state's vocabulary. Sitting with a party of men in a hotel lobby one evening, he was expressing his dislike for the country in many uncomplimentary terms, and wound up by remarking, 'No, gentlemen, Californy isn't in it with old Missoury. Why, they can't raise anything out here but alpaca, and they have to irritate that!' A year in one of the excellent public schools of this wonderful state would doubtless improve his knowledge in several particulars.

"Doubling back a few hundred miles, we visited the wonderful Yosemite Valley and the Mariposa big trees. Somebody, a globe-trotter, once said, 'See all the rest of the world before visiting Yosemite, for afterward everything else will seem tame in comparison.' You have been there, have you not, Doctor?"

"Yes," was the reply. "I spent a week there three summers ago."

"Then you will readily excuse me from attempting to describe this really indescribable place. When I saw the Multnomah Falls in Oregon, 850 feet high, I was speechless in admiration. But Multnomah is but a rivulet, a mere child's plaything, as compared with Yosemite, which seems to start in the clouds, 2,600 feet above.

"Leaving California, we plunged across the desert, a long, tedious ride. When at last we reached Salt Lake City, it was like coming out of a nightmare into the sunshine and sparkling dews of a June morning. We spent a day in the Mormon capital, visiting the great tabernacle and other places of interest. Running out to Garfield Beach in the afternoon, we all went bathing. It was rare sport, and no danger of drowning in this great inland sea, which is phenomenal in that it is almost one-fourth salt. However, salt or no salt, sister and I are both good swimmers, an exercise which I have greatly enjoyed for years as I have had opportunity. That's another of my new-woman ideas, Doctor; I think every lady should learn to swim. It is not only a healthful and exhilarating sport, but might sometimes prove a useful accomplishment."

"Agreed," said I. "Go on."

"I was glad to note that Gentile enterprise is at last dominating Utah, and that Mormonism promises to be a mere relic of the foolish past at no very distant day. How tolerant are the good people of our land! They will let anybody practice anything if they will only declare it to be their religion. This is not liberty, but license, and it is high time our statesmen were opening their eyes to some other evils as bad as polygamy.

"From Salt Lake City we proceeded into the Rockies proper. Up the Grand River, over Tennessee Pass and down the Arkansas we flew, drinking in the glorious scenery on every hand. We stopped an hour at the Royal Gorge, and in awe studied the lofty walls above us and the angry current beneath. Of course, we visited Manitou and the Garden of the Gods. Yes, and climbed Pike's Peak, that stalwart captain of them all. We entered the grand cavern and speculated on the age of stalagmites and stalactites like real scientists. We climbed, and climbed, and climbed, till each gained an appetite sufficiently ravenous to please the most ambitious health-seeker. It was a glorious trip from first to last, and now, lest I weary you, I will conclude by saying that we spent a day in Denver, the 'Queen City of the Plains,' and then sped homeward, crossing the much-abused state of Kansas, where there is more of the true, intelligent, patriotic reform spirit that you know I so much admire than in any other state of the Union."

"I have been delighted with your narrative," said I, "and you are certainly to be congratulated, not only for the opportunities afforded you by this trip, but for the excellent manner in which you improved the same."

We chatted on about other things for awhile, until I began to grow nervous. Not one word could I induce her to speak of Vincent by any of the subtle arts of conversation. I was almost dying to know whether they were engaged, and yet I did not dare ask her. Somehow I doubted it, and yet I was morally certain that this had been the railroad magnate's purpose in planning the trip.

"How well you look, Doctor!" said she, abruptly changing the tide of conversation. "It does me good to note your improvement."

"Yes," I replied, feeling somewhat flattered, and yet I knew that she was sincere. "I am as firm a bicycle fiend as you dare be now. And as to Indian clubs, rowing, putting the shot and all the other arts of working up muscle, color and appetite, I am almost a Sandow."

"Good!" said the dear girl, clapping her hands in unfeigned delight. "Speaking of Sandow, I've been told that he was once a weak man, inclined to consumption. But attention to the laws of health and perpetual exercise, has made him one of the strongest men of the age. Do you know, people would be better off if instead of running to the doctor with every little ill they would eat proper food, take proper exercise and bathe much in the pure oxygen of heaven's great outdoors. And we are advancing. More attention is being paid to these matters now than ever before. Already the average age of human life has increased three years the past ten. Another century of progress and it will be very common for people to live one hundred years and more."

Still nothing about Vincent. Oh, why did she not say something that would reveal the facts in the case? If I could only be assured that there was nothing between them I would propose at once, whether for weal or woe. But I hesitated.

She was attired in a suit of brown—brown bloomers, brown waist, brown hose and pretty little slippers tied with brown ribbon. She wore a bunch of forget-me-nots at her breast. All this I had observed a hundred times during the evening, and each time with increasing admiration. With my added strength had come greater love for this woman of all women to me, and I longed to fold her to my bosom and speak words of ardent love into those pretty ears which nestled, half hidden, beneath the rich folds of her beautiful hair. But I hesitated, thinking that that might be a privilege which belonged by right of conquest to a bolder man than I had been.

Glancing at my watch, I saw that it was almost time for the Browns to return, and remarked that I must be going. We chatted a few minutes longer and then I started. She accompanied me into the hall, where we lingered another ten minutes. As I looked down into those wondrous eyes I thought I detected my own image there, not as when one looks into a mirror, but as when you look into the soul of

one whose heart beats in unison with your own. For
a moment I was spell-bound. It seemed now that my
fond hopes must be fulfilled, and that I must clasp
her to my heart, smother her sweet face with kisses
and call her my own. But Vincent's ghost came to
mind. What if she had already promised him? Then
what a fool I would be!

"Oh, I came nearly forgetting to ask you how long
you intend tarrying in the city this time?" said I,
feeling that I should smother if I didn't say something.

"Only a day or two."

"Indeed! I'm sorry. I had hoped to see more of
you."

"Then accept my most cordial invitation to spend
the holidays at our home," said she. "You will need
a little rest again by that time, and we will all be delighted to have your company through the gala week
of the year."

"I will come," I said, surprised, flattered, filled
with a new hope.

I took her soft, warm hand in mine, and she was
not quick to withdraw it. Certainly she thinks more
of me than of him, I thought. And yet, perhaps, this
is one of her little arts to deceive—they may be engaged after all.

"Good night, and good-bye till Christmas."

DISAPPOINTMENT.

CHAPTER IX.

DISAPPOINTMENT.

"The best-laid schemes o' mice and men,
  Gang aft a-gley,
And leave us nought but grief and pain,
  For promised joy."
                                    —BURNS.

It was Thanksgiving evening. Grace Thorne and Sidney Vincent were seated in the library in the latter's home at Smithville. Vincent had arrived from Chicago the day before, and side-tracked his private car for three days' stop at the little Wisconsin town where lived the lady he loved above all others. He had been remarkably successful in his business deals for several months past and was now quoted among the millionaires in railroad circles. And still he was unmarried. He felt that the time had fully come for him to select a companion and establish a fashionable home. So calling his chief clerk into his private office, he quickly arranged matters for a short vacation, and then scribbled the following telegram:

Chicago, Nov. 27, 1896.
Miss Grace Thorne, Smithville, Wis.

Your gracious invitation to spend Thanksgiving accepted. Will come to-morrow.

SIDNEY VINCENT.

There was no special excitement at the Thorne residence over the expected guest, for they were hospitable people, and were always extending invitations to their friends, and among all their acquaintances none seemed more deserving of the favors of the season than Sidney Vincent, whose close attentions and innumerable kindnesses for six months past had made the whole family his debtors.

The forenoon after his arrival was a pleasant one. The sun shone brightly, and, in company with Miss Grace and her sister, the railroad magnate took a long drive. At two o'clock dinner was ready. Henry Thorne, with his wife and babies, had run up from St. Louis to eat turkey and pumpkin pie once again at the old home. Other relatives were present, and one or two of Josephine's school friends. It was a pleasant party, not too large, not too small, and everybody in the best of humor, as they should be on this blessed day.

After dinner came music, conversation, laughter and an all-round good time. During the afternoon the mercury had fallen twenty degrees and the wind soughed and moaned among the trees in a way to suggest most forcibly the advisability of staying indoors. The guests departed early, fearing a severe blizzard, and the man kindled crackling fires in the grates. Vincent and Miss Grace finally pre-empted the library, and, drawing chairs close to the fire, sat down for a quiet, uninterrupted chat.

"Miss Grace," began Vincent, with that keen business look in his steel-grey eyes which had so often pierced the motives of his associates on 'change to his advantage, "I have desired for a long time to speak with you on a subject that will concern you, I hope, as deeply as it does myself."

He stopped a moment to note the effect these words might produce. But the face of the lady remained unchanged. She met his glance squarely and innocently, as she calmly said:

"Proceed, Mr. Vincent. You are well aware of my weakness for talk. It is a common failing with my sex. Science has recently declared that this failing, if it must be called such, is owing to a difference in the brain tissues of man and woman. Be that as it may, I am ready to hear what you have to say, with interest and pleasure, I trust."

"I had thought to speak to you during our Western trip," he continued, in the same tone as before her philosophic reply, "but there were so many in the party, and our time so constantly occupied with sight-seeing when we were not at rest, that I had no good opportunity. Miss Thorne—Grace—since our first meeting in the city several months ago I have been infatuated with you and have long been waiting anxiously for the moment when I could declare my love. At last the moment has come, and I now offer you my all. Grace—darling—will you be my wife?"

He had arisen from his chair and knelt politely on one knee just beside her, and now held out his fat, jeweled hands imploringly. She did not scream, nor faint, but with slightly heightened color, which the keen-eyed Vincent thought greatly enhanced the beauty of her snowy neck and luscious cheeks, she quietly replied:

"Mr. Vincent, I trust you will not think me ungrateful, for I sincerely appreciate your every kindness and respect you as one of my dearest friends, but I cannot accept your gracious offer."

Non-plussed, astonished, dazed, the rich, confident, imperious man almost lost his self-control. Scores of anxious mothers in the swellest of swell circles in various cities had set their traps for him again and again, but all to no avail, for the present daughter was the only one he had ever seen for whom he cared enough to bow the knee. And now to think she refused! It was indeed stunning. But in a moment he regained his staggered composure and was as cool as if manipulating a gigantic deal in the interests of his corporation.

"Oh, Miss Thorne—Grace—dearest one—you do not refuse me! It cannot be possible that I have read your heart wrongly as I have time and again studied the expression of those charming eyes? Why can you not accept my offer, sweet lady? Is it because you do not love me?"

"That is the only reason a true woman dare sug-

HE HAD RISEN FROM HIS CHAIR, AND KNELT
POLITELY ON ONE KNEE, JUST BESIDE HER, AND
NOW HELD OUT HIS FAT JEWELED HANDS IM-
PLIRINGLY.—Page 224.

gest under such circumstances, Mr. Vincent," was the earnest reply.

"But why do you not love me?" he asked, almost petulantly.

"Take your seat again, Mr. Vincent, and I will tell you," she said.

Mortally chagrined, the haughty wooer seated himself again and remained at a respectable distance from the object of his affections, while she began calmly to analyze him to himself with a gentleness and directness most humiliating.

"In the first place, Mr. Vincent—and you will pardon me for speaking plainly, for I am your friend—because you are an infidel. While I do not pose as a saint, and know that my life is far from perfect, I am a believer in God and the Bible. I think Christ of Nazareth the world's only hope, and could never be happy with a husband who thought otherwise. These are great fundamental truths, and I feel that I would be risking my happiness here and my soul hereafter if I should accept your hand, knowing as I well know from your oft declared unbelief, that you have been a scoffer at all these things I hold sacred, for the greater part of your life."

"But, my dear Miss Thorne, I will gladly agree to hold my tongue forever on all these questions, and promise you upon my word and honor that your religious convictions shall never be impugned by me. Only be my wife, dearest Grace, and I will make you happy, if granting your every request will do it. But I confess that I do not believe in religion, and will not deceive you by promising that I will try to do so."

"Why do you not believe?" inquired the now fully aroused young lady. Her natural love for argument and investigation asserted itself, and, anyhow, she much preferred a battle with logic just now to a battle with disappointed love.

"Because I cannot," said Vincent.

"But that is an unsatisfactory answer, Mr. Vincent. Perhaps you have never tried. It is quite popular in certain circles nowadays to doubt, and I am positive that many persons are trying infinitely harder not to believe than they are to believe. It is a dangerous fad which has bred a vast litter of skeptical books, insipid addressess and free-and-easy society organizations. I surmise that it is a recoil from the ultra-orthodoxy of past generations; but because our ancestors were unwise in their adherence to certain inconsistent tenets it is no reason we should swing to an extreme of unfaith ten times more so. Christianity has met every test successfully for nearly two thousand years, and its own history is a vindication of its genuineness."

"How about the Dark Ages, Miss Thorne? Would you undertake to defend the horrors of the Inquisition, and the martyrdoms of a thousand years of church rule?"

"By no means. Every good thing is counterfeited, and the crimes enacted by a corrupt church should not be attributed to the religion of Jesus. Church-ianity and not Christianity is to blame for the blood of martyrs. The great trouble is that many do not wish to endorse the lofty principles of New Testament religion, for it would hurt their business. And so they read the depraved ranting of foul-mouthed agnosticism with a relish, thereby steeling their hearts against the gentle pleadings of the gospel. Nine professed infidels out of ten are woefully unfamiliar with the Bible; and as to standard works on Christian evidence, they do not care to know they exist."

"Oh, of course some kind of a religion is perhaps necessary," interjected Vincent, who was only too weary of the discussion; "but why not that of Buddha, or Confucius, Mohammed, or Zoroaster? Why insist on the Bible in preference to the Talmud or the Koran? So far as I have been able to see there is about as much truth in one as another."

"But the facts are against you, Mr. Vincent. The history of true civilization is the history of Christianity. All religions contain truth, some more, some less; but the Christian scriptures are the essence of all truth, for they reveal what no other sacred work does—man's real relationship to an Omnipotent, All-Wise and All-loving Being. Professor Lowber, in his great work entitled 'Cultura,' says: 'It is a fact that idolatrous nations have never been able to extricate themselves from idolatry. Truth had to be presented from without, and that truth was the gospel of Christ as contained in the Bible. You find no nation highly civilized which does not believe in the Bible. The Bible and civilization go together. Man is so constituted that he will worship, and he becomes assimilated to the character of that which he worships.'"

"But, Miss Grace," urged Vincent, "brilliant minds differ on these things. So why should you and I give ourselves such earnest concern about them until they are settled?"

"I grant you that brilliant minds differ," continued Miss Thorne, "but the really great minds of the world agree in favor of Christianity as against irreligion. Mr. Gladstone says: 'The greatest of all questions of the day is that of the gospel. It can and will correct everything needing correction. All men at the head of great movements are Christian men. During the many years I was cabinet officer I was brought in association with sixty master minds, and all but five of them were Christians.' Daniel Webster was once asked what was the greatest thought he ever had. He replied: 'My personal responsibility to a personal God.' When James Russell Lowell was our minister to England he was once present at a dinner in London when some of the speakers present expressed their contempt for Christianity, declaring that they could get along without it, and depreciating its influence upon men. Mr. Lowell volunteered a caustic reply to their sophistries, a portion of which, with your permission, I would like to read."

Stepping to the book shelves, Miss Thorne took therefrom a volume, and standing beneath the chandelier, quickly turned to the place she desired, and read the following words:

"I do not think it safe," said the distinguished poet, statesman and scholar. "I am formulating no creed of my own; I have always been a liberal thinker, and have, therefore, allowed others who differed from me to think also as they liked; but at the same time I fear that when we indulge ourselves in the amusement of going without a religion, we are not, perhaps, aware how much we are sustained at present by an enormous mass, all about us, of religious feeling and religious conviction; so that whatever it may be safe for us to think—for us who have had great advantages, and have been brought up in such a way that a certain moral direction has been given to our character—I do not know what would become of the less favored classes if they undertook to play the same game. The worst kind of a religion is no religion at all; and these men, living in ease and luxury, may be thankful that they live in a land where the gospel they neglect has tamed the beastliness and ferocity of the men who, but for

Christianity, might long ago have eaten their car-
casses like the South Sea Islanders, or cut off their
heads and tanned their hides like the monsters of
the French Revolution.

"When the microscopic search of skepticism,
which has hunted the heavens and sounded the seas
to disprove the existence of a Creator, has turned
its attention to human society, and has found a place
on this planet, ten miles square, where a decent man
can live in decency, comfort and security, supporting
and educating his children unspoiled and unpol-
luted; a place where age is reverenced, infancy protected, manhood respected, womanhood honored,
and human life held in due regard—when skepticism
finds such a place ten miles square on this globe
where the gospel of Christ has not gone and cleared
the way, and laid the foundations, and made decency
and security possible, it will then be in order for the
skeptical literati to move thither, and there ventilate
their views. But so long as these very men are de-
pendent upon the religion that they discard for
every privilege they enjoy, they may well hesitate
a little before they seek to rob the Christian of his
hope, and humanity of its faith in that Savior who
alone has given to man that hope of eternal life
which makes life tolerable and society possible, and
robs death of its terror and the grave of its gloom."

As she replaced the book, Vincent's eyes followed
her every movement with a longing inexpressible.

He had been more charmed with her reading than with what she read. Never had she seemed so queenly to him as now. He loved her with all the love a man of his sordid make-up could love, and felt that he could not possibly brook defeat in his purpose to have her his wife. Feeling that to argue with her was absolutely useless, he sought to change the tide of affairs by an appeal to vanity. She had resumed her seat and was looking thoughtfully at the cheerful fire when he began—

"I do not care to argue with you, Miss Grace, for on religious subjects you are clearly beyond my reach. I confess that I have never read the Bible through, and have given little attention to evidences of any kind, for or against Christianity. I have been a strictly business man for years, and have succeeded handsomely. Today I am rich, popular, powerful. I want a wife who is my equal and you are the only lady who can fill the bill. If you will accept me, my fortune is at your disposal, and I promise you that I will not hinder you in the exercise of any of your whims, social, political, or otherwise. This is no light matter, Miss Thorne, and I trust you will consider it with the good sense for which you are eminently noted. Mind you, my skepticism shall never be mentioned in your presence, and if that is your only objection, it seems to me that you ought to give me your hand right here and now."

And once again he assumed the attitude of petitioner, kneeling at her side, and gently soliciting her hand.

"But there are other objections, Mr. Vincent," said she.

"And pray, what can they be?" pleaded the now thoroughly awe-struck lover. To have been compelled to assume the defensive was a thing he had not expected nor prepared for.

"To be frank, yet I hope not unkind, Mr. Vincent, some of your personal habits. I would almost as soon be the wife of an infidel as to link myself for life with an habitual user of tobacco and strong liquors."

And she looked the astonished suitor squarely in the face, as his countenance changed from one expression to another and back again with a rapidity quite exciting.

"Why, Miss Thorne!" he implored. "I am astonished that your demands of a husband should be so excessively strict. It is true that I smoke just like other men, some better and some worse than myself, and that I occasionally partake of stimulants. How can one avoid it when in society? But what harm is there in sipping a little champagne, or, for that matter, in taking a little alcohol when over-burdened with work, as I am at times. But I have never been the worse from liquor and would scorn the thought of excess in that direction."

"Oh, certainly," remarked Miss Thorne, somewhat coolly, Vincent thought. "All moderate drinkers say the same. But it's all wrong. Liquor is a poison, and no human being is excusable for taking it into the stomach as a beverage under any circumstance whatever. Nor can it be done without injury to a greater or lesser extent. Though you can easily con-trol your appetite at present, the time might not be far distant when drinking would become a disease with you, and then my life, if I were your companion, would be miserable, no matter how elegant our home, nor how heavy our bank account."

"But your Bible says to take a little wine for the stomach's sake, does it not?" asked Vincent, think-ing to parry her blows somewhat.

"Certainly, and I should probably say the same thing under similar circumstances. The Apostle Paul was addressing a sickly young preacher and did right in recommending the pure, unfermented juice of the grape as a food and tonic for his jaded body. But if Timothy could have consumed a barrel of the kind of wine his superior recommended it would not have intoxicated him. Not so with your fer-mented champagnes and nineteenth century whisky."

"But I can easily give up liquor of every descrip-tion for you if necessary; I cannot understand why you should be so foolish about smoking, however, for it seems to me a simple, harmless habit, in which most men of all ranks and conditions indulge."

"Because," continued Miss Thorne, and every word

was like a dissecting knife to the man at her side, who had now resumed his seat, and who, chin in hand, was philosophically studying the hickory log in the glowing grate before him, "tobacco is also a poison, and nearly every reason that can be urged against the use of liquor can be urged against the use of tobacco. Both are narcotics of the worst type. The plant from which your cigars are made is one of the most deadly known to botany. No one can absorb nicotine into the system without bad results. Tobacco slowly murders its tens of thousands of victims every year and blights the lives of hundreds of thousands of others with disease. It causes paralysis, heart trouble, cancer of the throat, neurasthenia, dyspepsia, blindness, stunted growth, consumption, and time would fail me to name the multitude of evils created or augmented by the use of the obnoxious weed. Horace Greeley, speaking of the smell of tobacco smoke, once said: 'It is a profane stench.' And Webster facetiously remarked: 'If those men must smoke, let them take the horse shed.' 'Killed by too much cavendish' would be a far more appropriate epitaph for many tombstones than some of the exotic eulogies we see in every cemetery. Smoking pollutes the teeth and breath, dulls the mental faculties, inflames the baser nature, and wills to heredity an abnormal makeup which often dishonors a beneficent Creator."

"You ought to be a spectacled professor in some

ladies' college," was the only reply Vincent attempted, as a sickly smile crept over his features.

"Never," insisted Miss Thorne, "for I am a believer in co-education of the sexes."

"Another hobby?" asked Vincent, the smile slowly expanding.

"Yes, these new women of whom you read so much have many hobbies. The men have had it all their own way so long, however, that they ought not to object to us having a little of the sport, too, in these dissipated days. Especially when our hobbies are sensible, and make for the betterment of the race."

Vincent's smile now broke into a short, hoarse laugh. Then shifting his position a little, he coyly inquired:

"And have you any other objections to your adorer?"

"Yes, Mr. Vincent," she replied, "it is one not often urged in this material age, and yet it is of vast importance with me. You love money too well."

"That is indeed a strange objection for a woman to urge against a prospective husband," said Vincent. "Money seems to be the chief requirement with most women, and it is certainly a very useful adjunct to married life. I know your Bible says that money is the root of all evil, or something to that effect; but I have observed that most church members dig for it about as anxiously as we wicked men of the world. You seem to be an all-round exception, however." And he coughed a little cynical, business-like cough.

"No, Mr. Vincent, the Bible does not say a word against money. It says that the love of money is the root of all evil. That's a very different thing. Money is power, and I rejoice to see it accumulated in the hands of generous, philanthropic persons. But when money is amassed simply for money's sake, it becomes a curse. Milton spoke incisively when he wrote:

'Mammon led them on,
Mammon, the least erected spirit that fell
From heaven.'

It is painful to witness the terrible scramble for gold to-day. Men of every rank and station in life have been led into the struggle, so fascinating has it become. It is a mania which shuts out all growth in other directions, fostering selfishness, deceit, cruelty. Hood very aptly described the present condition of things in America when he wrote:

'Gold, gold, gold, gold,
Bright and heavy, hard and cold,
Molten, graven, hammered, and rolled;
Heavy to get and light to hold;
Hoarded, bartered, bought and sold;
Stolen, borrowed, squandered, doled;
Spurned by the young, but hugged by the old
To the very verge of the church-yard mold;
Price of many a crime untold,—
Gold, gold, gold, gold.'

The great Master said: 'Ye cannot serve God and Mammon,' and so many men with one accord seem in these days to be choosing the latter."

"But have I not been liberal with my money?" inquired Vincent, apparently somewhat hurt.

"Oh, yes! With yourself and those you admire. Personally I shall never be able to repay your many kindnesses. But you have not been liberal with the poor and needy around you. There are hundreds of poor fellows working on your lines for a scanty nine dollars a week, and a family of four, six or nine to support. And yet twice a year your stockholders meet and declare mighty dividends. In your own city are thousands who do not know the meaning of good clothes and a square meal from one year's end to another, and yet your name has never appeared in the lists of public benefactors. By your own admission to me in a conversation held some months ago, these constant appeals on the part of philanthropic schemers fatigue you, and you generally instruct your clerk to tell them you are out when they call on you for donations. Out of a vast income you give but a mere pittance to lift up the fallen, when you could easily found a hospital, endow an industrial school, and establish a friendliness between capital and labor as it comes under your control which would bring joy to the burdened hearts of thousands. Hence I could never consent to be your wife and live at ease and in luxury, while I realized that others less favored deserved the money all this cost much more than I."

"And what else?" asked the millionaire, apparently anxious to conclude the examination. "Have you any other reason for refusing my offer? I may as well know them all."

"You are too old, Mr. Vincent," said she sweetly. "While I am but twenty-five, you are forty-one. A difference of sixteen years is too great in the marriage relation. I am aware that in many instances where the difference has been even greater the couple has gotten along nicely, to all appearances. But it is unnatural, and what is unnatural is unwise. You should prefer a wife nearer your own age. In fact, you should have married fifteen years ago. All this talk about marriage being a failure has been provoked by unnatural marriages. Persons rush into this, the most sacred relation of life, without due thought or preparation, and the result is unhappiness, and the institution itself is blamed when the silly incumbents ought to be. Wealth, blood, fame, and such like elements should always be considered secondary in the choice of a partner for life. Love should rule. Love marriages are the great need of the hour."

The fire had burned low, and the room was becoming chilly. The hands on the mantel clock pointed the hour of eleven. Vincent felt that he must now bring this unsatisfactory discussion to a close, and resolved to make one last, frantic effort. "The third time's the charm," he thought, as once again he knelt at Miss Thorne's feet.

"Grace—darling—pride of my heart and life—I cannot live without you. Do not cast me off. Help me to be the man you would have me to be. Become my wife and I will endeavor to conform to your every ideal. Refuse me, and I cannot vouch for the consequences."

And he took her hand in his and pressed it to his lips before she had time to answer. But gently withdrawing it, she quietly answered :

"Mr. Vincent, the worst policy a woman could possibly pursue is to marry any man to reform him. Many have tried it, and not one in ten thousand ever completes the task. There are worse men than you, a hundred times over. I shall be glad to count you among my warmest friends while life lasts if you will let me, but marry you I cannot. There is one reason I have kept till the last, and which I think will move you to retreat in this vain pursuit."

"One more?" exclaimed Vincent. "And tell me, what can it be?"

"My heart is not my own. I love another man."

UNDER THE MISTLETOE.

CHAPTER X.

UNDER THE MISTLETOE.

"I rest content; I kiss your eyes,
 I kiss your hair in my delight:
 I kiss my hand and say, 'Good-night.'"
                    —JOAQUIN MILLER.

   "She was good as she was fair,
     None—none on earth above her!
     As pure in thought as angels are,
     To know her was to love her."
                    —ROGERS.

Sidney Vincent did not stay three days. He left the following morning for Milwaukee, where he visited twenty-four hours at the home of a millionaire brewer and proposed to his youngest daughter, a butterfly maiden of nineteen summers. Of course, he was accepted, for he was a warm acquaintance of the old gentleman and had attended several fashionable receptions at his home in bygone days. For several years it had been one of the fondest dreams of Mrs. Millionaire Brewer to marry her Miss Isabel to this wealthy and popular railroad magnate. So arrangements were promptly effected, and the affair set for Christmas-tide. It was considered a royal match by the gossips, for it enhanced the wealth and worldly prospects of both sides in the bargain and insured to society another aristocratic establishment.

All this, and much more, I learned upon good authority some time after it occurred. Well, generally speaking, folks are sooner or later assorted according to affinity, and it is quite proper.

As the holidays approached I could scarcely wait for the hour of my departure for Smithville. Several friendly letters had passed between myself and Miss Thorne. But as yet I was no wiser than I had been concerning the real status of affairs between herself and Vincent. Nor was Mrs. Brown. Although a most intimate friend of the latter's, the fair young lady had never divulged her intentions matrimonially. She was a wise general who kept her own counsel in this matter.

"But I cannot believe that Miss Grace will ever marry Mr. Vincent," said the banker's wife one day as we were talking over the subject. "She will marry whom she loves when she does marry, and I have never heard her say anything which would warrant one in concluding that she loved the railroad man."

This gave me hope, and I firmly resolved that I would not return from her sweet presence this trip without knowing my fate. Time did not lessen my love for her, but it seemed to deepen, heighten, broaden with each passing day and hour. I felt that no other could ever take her place in my affections, and often wondered what would become of me

if after all she should wed Vincent. I longed to
settle the question forever; and yet I feared the outcome. As Madame de Stael says, "Where we really
love, we often dread more than we desire the solemn
moment that exchanges hope for certainty." And
Sir Philip Sidney spoke truthfully when he said:
"They love indeed who quake to say they love."

At last I was on the way. A heavy snow had fallen
the night previous and my train was two hours late
in reaching Smithville. But Miss Grace and her
good father were at the depot awaiting my arrival.
This surprised me almost as much as it pleased me,
for the hour was well into the night.

"We are happy to welcome you again, Doctor,"
said Miss Thorne, as she extended her little gloved
hand, warmly. "And you are looking so well."

"Yes," I replied, more than pleased, "I am in perfect health. Of course, I find the Thornes all well,
for it is the natural order of things?"

"Exactly," remarked Mr. Thorne, as he drew a
heavy robe about us and gave the mare a gentle cut.

They had come for me in a sleigh. It was a crisp,
starry night, and as we skimmed over the snow to the
merry jingle of bells I felt with Tennyson that

"Love could walk with banished Hope no more."

After a cup of hot water, a piece of buttered toast
and a half hour's conversation, I retired. The next
forenoon was spent in pleasant visitation, and the
afternoon in sleigh riding. We drove out to the villa

and made an interesting call on the old butler and his wife. Jim was present, and at my request favored me with a couple of games at checkers, in both of which he worsted me ignominiously, and then added insult to injury by saying:

"Revner, if you can't preech better'n you play checkers, I pity the folks as comes to hear yer!"

The hearty laugh which followed was entirely at my expense, and I only partially parried the attack by asking Jim if he had seen the ghost at Myers' bridge lately. Aunt Martha insisted on us remaining to dinner, saying that she had on a Christmas goose. But we excused ourselves on account of Miss Grace having an engagement at the church that evening. The Sunday-school had an old-fashioned Christmas tree, and she promised her boys to be present. She kept her promise and saw that each of them received a handsome and useful gift. I accompanied her to the services, and was never more pleased with the dear girl than on this occasion, when her face fairly shone with delight as she moved here and there among the happy throng, adding little touches to the arrangements, without which the exercises of the hour would have been much less successful.

"To-morrow we will make some calls," she said as we walked home. "You remember that I promised you once that you might accompany me on one of my rounds among the poor. I would not think of making

ONE OF THE MANY HOMES IN SMITHVILLE WHERE
MISS THORNE IS A WELCOME VISITOR.

such a proposition to others at this gala season, but I know your interest in this sort of work."

"Yes, Miss Grace, I shall be only too glad to go with you," I assured her. "When we are most happy ourselves we should be the more willing to share it with others less fortunate; and as Christmas comes but once a year, those who can should make it mean much to the sorrow-stricken and downcast about them."

During the day Miss Josephine had decorated the Thorne home with mistletoe and holly and Mrs. Thorne and Bridget had prepared a wealth of tempting delicacies for the morrow's spread. It was almost midnight when we all retired, after a jolly evening in the best room. The girls played and sang, the man made some cider and brought it fresh from the press, ice cold, and little eight-year-old Nellie, who had come from the city to spend holidays with grandpa and grandma, spoke a piece or two. Then the head of the household took down the old Book and read Luke's account of the Saviour's birth, and we all knelt in prayer. In a few well-chosen words he thanked the Father for the many blessings of the hour, petitioned mercy for the poor and needy everywhere and committed the souls of all to His tender care. There was nothing stiff about it, but a simple, sweet, devotional spirit that charmed me beyond expression. Verily, I thought, David was right when he said: "The ways of religion are the ways of pleasantness."

Enjoying the pleasures of such a fireside, my muse was thoroughly aroused, and I found it difficult to sleep for an hour or more after retiring. I thought of Mulock's words:

"It is the Christmas time;
  And up and down 'twixt heaven and earth,
  In the glorious grief and solemn mirth,
  The shining angels climb."

It was quite late the following morning when Miss Thorne and I started out for twenty calls among the poor. But it was a bright day, and our hearts were light. The man drove us about in a double-seated sleigh, in which had been packed twenty baskets, each filled with good things. There was no formality about this self-appointed missionary's calls. She went into the homes of her flock like a sunbeam. It was:

"Good morning, Mrs. Muggins! How are you? And how is that dear little baby and the rest of the children? A merry Christmas to you all!"

Or,

"Hello, Bobby! Hello, Sally! Did Old Santa Claus bring you anything this year? What, no! Then we'll see about that. Ho, there, William (calling to the man), bring in that little basket, please."

And everywhere she was royally welcomed. Sad-faced mothers brightened up, and ragged children fairly danced with glee as she opened up the bas-

UNDER THE MISTLETOE.

kets and dispensed gifts which she had thoughtfully provided for one and all.

As we drove from place to place, some of the church bells rang, and a number of well-dressed, cultured-looking people might be seen wending their respective ways to the church of their choice. Whereupon Miss Thorne remarked:

"It is all very nice for those to go to church this morning who have been abundantly blessed with the good things of this life; but somebody must think of the poor unfortunates. But I do love to hear the bells. It reminds me of one of Longfellow's stanzas:

'I heard the bells on Christmas Day
Their old, familiar carols play,
And wild and sweet
The words repeat
Of peace on earth, good-will to men!'

And, yet, Doctor, there is so much formality about our churches to-day. It keeps the masses out. When will our spiritual leaders learn that acceptable service of God does not consist in conforming to certain ritualisms, and in always doing the same thing in the same stiff way; but in fulfilling the law of Christ, the crowning principle of which is love. To my mind the greatest verse in the New Testament is this: 'Inasmuch as ye have done it unto one of the least of these, my brethren, ye have done it unto me.' He best serves God who best serves humanity. The Bible tells us how."

And thus she chatted on, throwing out here and there nuggets of golden truth which would have done credit to the profoundest thinkers of history. She had certainly been much with books, and yet she was not bookish at all. Mingling daily with the great work-a-day world about her, she had kept her brilliant mind and sympathetic heart free from cobwebs and moss.

It was a merry Christmas dinner indeed that we sat down to at two o'clock. Six courses, interspersed with hearty good cheer made the hour one long to be remembered.

"Let's go skating!" suggested Miss Josephine, as we arose from the table.

"What do you say, Doctor?" asked Miss Grace. "I'm willing."

"I should enjoy going," said I.

And we were soon off. The man drove us over to the lake at the villa, where the skating was excellent. It was one of my favorite sports, as it seemed to be with the girls, and we spent two very pleasant hours at it.

Returning home by dusk, I was left alone awhile. Throwing myself into the big easy chair in the parlor, where I had so often sat before, I wondered whether the terrible suspense I was undergoing would ever come to a satisfactory end. Two days had passed, and not a word on the subject nearest my heart. Vincent's name had not been mentioned,

THE SKATING WAS EXCELLENT.—Page 256.

which appeared to me a favorable omen, for, I reasoned, if she were engaged to him, she could not
keep it, strong-minded and cautious though she be.

Presently the object of my long, heartfelt study
came in, attired, as ever, in bloomers. During the
day she had worn a navy blue suit, heavy and warm,
with leggins and cape to match. Miss Josephine
had worn a suit of brown, similarly made, and was
almost as fascinating as her sister. As we skated I
remarked more than once the eminent superiority of
such a costume for the exercise we were enjoying
over the old, troublesome skirts.

Miss Grace had gone to her room upon our return
and exchanged the navy blue for a lighter suit of
plaited creton. The waist was cut lower in the neck
than usual, revealing just a little of her plump square
shoulders and broad, well-rounded chest, which a
little gold chain and sparkling pendant set off most
winsomely. The sleeves were large and open, suggesting ease and good fellowship. There were no
leggins over the thick, firmly-knit dark hose, and
her boots had given place to a pair of slippers that
for ease and beauty combined would have made Cin-
derella wild. The hair had been rearranged, and
from head to foot she now appeared to me more than
ever before a dream of womanly perfection.

"Papa and mamma have gone out for the evening,"
she said, as she closed the door and drew the low
divan a little nearer the grate, "and sister has re-

tired to her room to write some letters. So I guess you and I will be obliged to entertain ourselves as best we can, Doctor."

"Well, Miss Thorne, I think we are equal to the emergency, do you not?" I asked, as I drew my chair a little nearer the fire, and in easy conversing distance.

We talked of books, music and the various reforms as usual, concluding with divorce. On this subject Miss Grace was very pronounced.

"It is a shame," she said, "that the divorce laws of our country are so loose. Why, in Missouri, I am told, there are eleven different legal loop-holes for separation. There are thirty thousand divorces a year in the United States. Chicago alone contributes nearly 1,000 to this list. No wonder marriage is considered a failure by some disappointed old bachelors and spinsters and wrecked mariners on the matrimonial sea. Swift says, 'The reason why so many marriages are unhappy is because young ladies spend their time in making nets, not in making cakes.' But he should not have omitted to score the other side by suggesting that club life among men often sours the taste for a natural and felicitous domesticity. Tennyson declares that

'Marriages are made in heaven.'

This is true of genuine love marriages, perhaps, but not of all matrimonial contracts, for many are made in the counting room in this practical age."

BUCKINGHAM PALACE—HOME OF QUEEN VICTORIA.

She stopped, and, looking me pleasantly in the face, seemed to be waiting for me to say something. My heart fluttered, and the blood must have rushed to my cheeks, for I felt them tingling as I endeavored to reply. It was awkward, but I said:

"But you are theorizing. Possibly you may marry some day yourself, and find things very much as others do after the honeymoon. Or, do you ever expect to marry—what is the doctrine of the new woman on this question?"

"Indeed, I hope to marry, for to wed and bring up children is the highest mission of womankind."

Again she paused, and I felt that my time had come. But I hesitated. Oh, tongue! Why art thou silent? said my heart. Why do you not speak your love, for willing ears await your burning words.

But I could not speak. In my pulpit, or in the social circle I had never been known to lack for words; but in the presence of this heavenly creature I had often found myself speechless. The silence was dreadful to me, and I was glad when she broke it again by a simple little question, simply put:

"Do you ever expect to marry, Doctor?"

My heart beat so powerfully that I feared she would hear it, and my face was growing so red that I instinctively turned it slightly away from her steady gaze as I answered, meekly:

"It is my fondest ambition."

Scarcely had the words left my lips till she shot another question more terrible than all the rest:

"Who?"

Now I knew my time had come, and I fairly clutched the arms of my big chair as I tried to frame a reply. Now or never! said a voice within. But again I hesitated, and possibly would have been a lonely wanderer in some unknown land to-day had not Grace Thorne had the good sense and courage to throw custom to the winds, break over all restraint, and act upon her better impulse by answering for me:

"Me, of course. Doctor, I love you, and know that you have loved me this long, long time. But brave and good as you are in all other things, you are timid in this. Hence my boldness. Do you want my hand?"

It seemed for a moment that a thousand electric wires had been wrapped about me, and a mighty current turned on. Arising from my chair, I took the sweetly proffered hand, and, sitting beside her on the low divan, broke forth in expressions of love and gratitude certainly sufficiently pronounced to meet all demands.

"A thousand times YES, Miss Thorne—Grace—darling one. Oh, how good you are, how brave and true! I thought perhaps you loved Vincent, and hence have delayed speaking to you on this subject for, lo, these many months. But I have loved you

FULLY ONE-HALF THE WOMEN NOW WEAR
BLOOMERS.—Page 271.

almost from the first with a love unspeakable. But can you really love me?"

Her answer was easily discernable as she gave me a look of infinite trust, and framed her pretty mouth for a kiss. Our lips met—once, twice, thrice, lingering longer together each time in a rapture transcendently blissful. It seemed that we had been caught up to the third heaven, so happy were we. My arm stole slyly around her yielding waist, and I pressed her close to my heart. As I did so her beautiful head nestled fondly on my breast, and I kissed her very hair in mad delight.

I do not know how long we continued so. It may have been ten minutes, and it may have been an hour. We talked little, for, as Havergal says,

"Love understands love, it needs no talk."

The moments were steeped in bliss, and each passionate touch of curl and dimple only added to my joy.

At last she gently withdrew from my arms, and, sitting hand in hand, we told the old, old story. Pointing to the mistletoe which hung just above our heads, she said:

"I had all this in view when I drew the divan so close to the grate this evening, Doctor."

"Call me Frank, please, darling," said I.

"Well, dear, old, timid Frank, then," she said, with a merry twinkle in her eyes, and a warmer press of the hand, "I've loved you a long time, you precious boy, and could not await your tardy declaration any longer."

"You are a brave, sweet girl. I feel unworthy of you, indeed I do. But, oh, how I do love you! And how happy I am! I now feel with Bayard Taylor what I have never felt before that

'Love is rest.'

And do you really love me, Grace?"

"Yes, Frank; in the language of the same poet, I can truly say,

'I love thee, I love but thee,
With a love that shall not die
  Till the sun grows cold,
  And the stars are old,
And the leaves of the Judgment Book unfold.'"

Twice the fire had to be replenished, as we talked and loved, and loved and talked. It was long after midnight when we said "Good night" at the foot of the stairs, with many a fond embrace and nectarine kiss.

* * * * * * * * * * *

We were married the following May. In the interim we paid each other several visits, I running out to Smithville occasionally and she running into the city. Mrs. Brown was almost beside herself with delight and she was closely seconded by the

FRANK, JUNIOR, AND GRACE, THE YOUNGEST.—
Page 272.

banker himself. The Thornes were all favorable to the union, and my people soon became reconciled to bloomers, and were as happy as the rest.

After the wedding we began housekeeping immediately, and spent our honeymoon in the bosom of our parish, which grew more prosperous every day. Neither of us favored a honeymoon trip, another curse which fashion has inflicted upon a long-suffering world. But after twelve months spent quietly at home, getting well and happily acquainted with each other, we went abroad for six months, visiting almost every place of interest in the Old World, and especially the city of London, the home of Queen Victoria.

* * * * * * * * * *

Five years have rolled by. Our church now numbers over three thousand members, thoroughly organized on the institutional plan, and constantly extending its influence for good. Mrs. Charlton still lectures occasionally, and is president of the American Dress Reform Society, which now has branches in almost every city and town on the continent. Fully one-half of the women of the land now wear bloomers, and the other half cannot hold out much longer. Bicycling is as common among women as walking, and many specialists in diseases peculiar to women have been compelled to quit their profession and go to farming for a living. Silver was restored in '96 and equal suffrage granted by voice of the people in 1900. The tariff question has been settled by the appointment of a bureau of non-partisan experts, and the liquor question is to be the chief bone of contention in 1904. Already the battle is being set in array, with every prospect of a sweeping victory for the advocates of national prohibition. Times are good, the people of the land are becoming more reverent, and America promises to be more than ever before a "missionary among the nations," diffusing light, liberty and love.

Two little ones have come to bless our home— Frank, junior, and Grace, the younger. Sometimes the busy cares of life almost o'erwhelm the soul, but an hour in the bosom of my little family after the day's work is done dispels every mist, and a thousand times I have thanked heaven for that sweet NEW WOMAN, who still wears bloomers, keeps abreast of the world's development, and proves to all by a wide-awake, up-to-date, whole-hearted devotion to principle that life is worth living. Daily in our home is verified the words of Longfellow:

> "As unto the bow the cord is,
> So unto the man is woman:
> Though she bends him, she obeys him;
> Though she draws him, yet she follows;
> Useless each without the other!"

THE END.

www.ingramcontent.com/pod-product-compliance
Lightning Source LLC
Chambersburg PA
CBHW020350030726
47496CB00007B/2080